MY THIEVERY OF THE PEOPLE

LEILA MARSHY

MY THIEVERY OF THE PEOPLE

Stories

Baraka Books
Montréal

ISBN 978-1-77186-377-3 pbk; 978-1-77186-383-4 epub; 978-1-77186-384-1 pdf

Cover by Leila Marshy
Book Design by Folio infographie
Editing: Elise Moser
Proofreading: Anne Marie Marko

Legal Deposit, 1st quarter 2025
Bibliothèque et Archives nationales du Québec
Library and Archives Canada

Published by Baraka Books of Montreal
Printed and bound in Quebec

TRADE DISTRIBUTION & RETURNS

Canada
UTPdistribution.com

United States
Independent Publishers Group: IPGbook.com

We acknowledge the support from the Société de développement des entreprises culturelles (SODEC) and the Government of Quebec tax credit for book publishing administered by SODEC.

SODEC Québec

Funded by the Government of Canada
Financé par le gouvernement du Canada
Canada

CONTENTS

BLINK TWICE

She was in a permanent state of self-protection, which meant she smiled a lot. It's hard to get close to someone who smiles all the time. Or maybe it's better to say there are two types of smiles, and hers was the type that kept you at bay.

"Blink twice," I said.

She looked up from the paper plate she was filling with vegetables and crackers. "Excuse me?" Her eyes, already tarry and unknowable, grew flinty. But the smile did not change.

"Oh sorry," I laughed, now a little unsteady on my otherwise well planted feet. "*Blink twice if you need to be rescued*. You know. That old saying."

"Oh okay. I guess it is older than me." She stopped smiling only long enough to pop a cherry tomato in her mouth. It was tasteless, I already knew that. All the food here was trucked into the city from god knows where, crammed into large plastic trays, and deposited on dusty tables where books had been shoved to the side. But it gave me a chance to see her face at rest, an austere carapace set in well-oiled leather.

"I'm not up on the latest lingo," she added.

"It's not really lingo." Her gaze was unrelenting, like it demanded a confession, an admittance of guilt. "It's what you say when you think someone needs help but can't articulate it for some reason." I blurted this too quickly.

Her smile creased harder in response, so I had to laugh louder to compensate. That's the thing about my laughter. If she had eaten another tomato or some of that terrible cheese, she would have seen that my laughter was just like her smile: it obfuscated, deflected and masked. Both our responses were armour. They were fully engaged in the denial of trauma and the cloaking of shame. In this state we could go forward and face the day with a modicum of bravado. We could look at each other's weaponry and trade metaphors of hidden jabs and unforeseen ambushes. My laughter and her smile; it was a great combination when you think about it.

She put the plate down and looked at me with intent, then blinked twice. But before I could say anything, a smile rounded across her face like a runaway train and I laughed like a possessed locomotive.

Anyone watching us would think we were having the time of our lives.

EVIDENCE OF MY THIEVERY OF THE PEOPLE

I was born to a man with thick hands. Hands that crumpled paper, signed paper, crumpled it again, threw it at faces darker than his own. This man caught my body pouring out of another, signed some papers, and took me home.

My bassinet sat in the vault and when I cried the papers rustled and that's how he knew I was there. He fed me ink and taught me to sign my name before I could walk. My mother? There were rumours, there was coffee. That is all I knew.

In a voice that scraped iron against iron, he boasted that our name meant *conqueror* and that if I wanted to feel his muscles, I could pay him with my allowance. This, he said, ensured that I was always profitable.

As the only son, my father's business fell into my lap like a prostitute's face. I burst through the door on a hot morning to see all eyes lower and the machines turn on again. My feet on the tiles prompted the clickings of "yes sir, yes sir, yes sir." I sat in a chair that could hold a family of four. My long fingers counted money with a reptilian finesse. Machines rolled and hummed in the background, filling the air with an acrid dust that sparkled like jewels, that made some of us rich and everyone else ill.

She came to my office on a Tuesday. Her face was new but the dress was the same, the dress her mother had worn when she brought my father coffee. My father roared when the new girl exited the room backwards, head down, apologizing. He laughed and slapped me on the back. His touch was painful. He yelled out for more coffee. Again and again. I stayed awake all night thinking of the dress, because when she left the room like that, hand reaching behind searching for the door, I noticed that the hem was torn. She seemed to live in the cupboard, preparing coffee after coffee for my father and, I noticed one day, tea for herself. She sometimes secretly hit me on the head. It was the only time she allowed herself to touch me. I took pleasure in these encounters.

She came to my office again on Wednesday. And on Thursday. That dress. How many times a week could she wear it? It was so much like the mother's. I wanted to talk to her. When she returned on Monday, I looked at her knees and said, "I see you've sewn the hem." I laughed a hearty laugh and slapped myself on the thigh. Her eyes dove to the seam, her free hand patting at the fabric with flustered movements. She made some noises, indecipherable words that I cannot recall. Sounds I am incapable of translating, perhaps because they were sincere.

Coffee is too strong. It is too black. It is bottomless. I hate it. I lie awake at night and it boils up from my stomach, pummelling my head in disgust.

I drink less than my father, so to fill her free time I gave her paperwork. It became a pleasure to know that both her hands were busy serving me: coffee and paper, coffee and paper. I offered her a cup one day. I insisted she drink it. I insisted. *Drink.* We sipped together. I stared at her face. I could not shake the feeling that it was her forehead, her nose, that I saw in the mornings when I shaved. She looked only at her knees. In between tastes she rested her cup on the edge of my desk. On the very edge, the bottom sticking out over the floor, as if to push it all the way in was presumptuous. I liked that. She spoke softly, "Thank you for the coffee, sir. Have a nice evening." Our voices shared the same timbre, but hers was fearful. I opened the door for her. I made sure she saw the slipping of my eyelids, saw them falling over her shoulders, her breasts, her belly, down her hips and around her bottom. The door shut as my gaze dripped down her legs.

By then the coffee was drunk and it was too late.

I dreamt of donkeys and waves of sand through which we, the donkeys and I, ran. They sang and suddenly I understood them. The horror of it! I covered my ears but still I heard it. They sang in her mother's voice. I am afraid she can hear. I am afraid she is listening.

The next day at my desk I called for coffee. Waited. Ten minutes passed; she should have arrived. I opened the door. Faces glanced up then quickly down again. I yelled at a young clerk. "You! Come here!" He dropped a stack of envelopes and came running.

"Yes sir, Accounting." My father didn't care for names, he only wanted departments. "And sometimes Mailroom. I began as Mailroom and then a little bit Administration but not long, now it is half..."

"Enough! Where is she?"

"Who, sir?"

"*Her*, dammit. Typing. No, Filing. No, Stenographer. Coffee. The coffee girl. I don't know—where the hell is that girl?"

"Do you mean Kitchen? I didn't see her today, sir. She's been sick, I do know that."

I hit him with my rolled-up papers. "Sick? What do you mean sick? She comes here every day for, for..."

"I don't know, sir, I just heard some things."

"What did you hear?"

"I don't know, sir, she went to see a doctor. Maybe she has the same thing her mother had."

My feet ground into the carpet. It was old and torn and I felt it ripping further. It occurred to me that it had been weeks since she wore that dress. "What did her mother have?"

"I don't know, sir. Some disease. Terrible. She was dying for months."

"Go. No, wait," I thrust a couple of bills into his hand. "Get me her address. Now. Before the end of the day. Tell no one."

My father had ordered me never to enter her neighbourhood. There were whispers when I was a child. Fever, blisters, boils, smells. Had she inherited a legacy of penance for the sins of her mother? Strange, I almost said *father.*

When I ventured there, I was relieved to have dressed down. No silks, no Italian shoes or fine woven hat. Perhaps I should not have brought the Mercedes, or at least could have driven it myself. Or maybe it was the keychain glinting in the sun, jangling in my hand like gold coins. Because as my feet touched the dung-scraped dirt of her street, hordes of ashen children set upon me shouting unintelligibly, thrusting their tiny paws onto my chest. I threw them a pen. A bit of change. Finally, noticing that my clothes were in danger of being soiled, I grabbed the smallest and wrapped my fingers around his throat. He kicked valiantly as I lifted his feet off the dirt. I threatened his friends: "I'll crush him!" They were silent, eyes piercing. I threw the boy to the ground. "Get out of my way!" He wriggled towards his friends before my foot could reach his stomach; he must have moved fast, because there was a great man's force behind that foot.

I found her house. In more glorious times the homes on her street had boasted painted porches and windows with glass panes and hot water in every kitchen. But the sidewalks had given way to gutters and every wall was cracked with rot. An old cat whose pregnant belly swept the gravel rubbed up against me and, braiding itself between my moving feet, hurled me forward on all fours. I clawed and screamed after the disgusting beast. Had I caught her, she and her offspring would have been dead. In front of me a door opened a crack and then shut in a hurry. I brushed myself off. The door opened again, and an old woman's eyes peered at me. I did not like her expression and this time I shoved my foot inside and prevented her from closing it. I entered the house.

An odour accosted me that was part heat, part rot, the rest flowers. The latter puzzled me until my eyes adjusted and I could see a cluster of wild blooms, yellow and purple, that had been recently gathered. Who had left them? I suppressed an urge to chase after shadows and smell their hands. Instead, I snatched up the bouquet and opened the window to throw it outside.

The old woman came running. Shouting, she slapped my hands and retrieved the vase. The insolence of her attack was startling. I shoved her away. As I opened the door to the girl's room, the only other room in the small house, a clay jar crashed against the wall behind me.

The bed was at the far corner. Her head was tilted softly to one side, as if ready for my arrival. Funny, I almost said *return*. The tinny sound of cars and children squeezed through the shutters and then, in the thick air of the room, fell like cinders to the floor. An elongated ridge between her chin and her toes bore through the coverlet like a snake. I stood beside her and was surprised to see that my breathing began to follow the rhythm of her chest.

I did not know why I was there.

I called to the old woman. "Do you have coffee?" She snorted but went to the small stove where I knew she would get quickly to work. She returned and placed a hot glass in my hands.

The girl opened her eyes. Her face registered surprise, followed by a flicker of panic. I attempted my harshest smile. She looked at me with an expression I did not recognize and that she held onto with determination. It pulled at me like a hardening scar. I broke eye contact.

"You have been sick for a long time," I said.

"Are you in very much pain?" I asked her.

"Your aunty has made me coffee," I told her.

"She is your aunty, too."

Her voice sparked through the air threatening to light it on fire. I could not be sure of what she said.

What is she talking about, I heard myself ask in the voice of my father. How dare she!

"She is our mother's sister. Our mother, who died from overwork and sadness. As I am dying." She closed her eyes briefly, opened them again, this time they were sharper. "As our father is dying. As you will die."

I backed up. I did not come here for this!

"I knew you would come," she said.

"How dare you."

She shrugged her shoulders. I stepped to the window and leaned against it, peered through the wooden slits. They were covered with dust, and it choked me till I coughed in dry spasms.

"See," she said even more softly, "now you are dying too."

"I am not dying!" I coughed again. "Your damned house is filthy." But the words scraped against my throat and I had to bend over again, then again. The coughing ripped through my insides, burst out into the corners of the room, took up residence under the bed. The contrails of dust blinded me, made me dizzy, settled on my eyes and mouth like a wet cloth of dirt. Even the old woman poked her head in.

"This is how our mother died," the girl said.

"From what? A dirty house? You are hallucinating."

She shrugged and closed her eyes. I wanted to wrap my fingers around her throat and crush her like the stupid creature in the alley. Such insolent nonsense! I came here like this and look at her—look at her! My father would never let such a thing happen.

"You have missed too much work," I said instead. "I have come here to—to fire you."

She made no move to indicate she had heard. Perhaps she slept? I leaned closer and prepared to speak louder. But her lips curled slowly up, like a hunter's bow, and a rustling sound emerged from her throat.

"You are laughing," I said, incredulous. "You are laughing."

Her face was mirthful, the laughter melodious and warm. I stepped in closer. She opened her eyes. "Sit on the bed, brother."

I could only obey. The girl took my hand in hers. She pursed her lips, "I would like a coffee."

I looked to the door for the old woman but she had disappeared. Who was to get this invalid her coffee?

"Please," she said, her voice hoarse.

Strangely compelled, I went to the stove and found what I needed to complete the task. The space was barely larger than a cupboard. I waited for the water to boil. Suddenly, I could smell the dress. For a brief moment I heard the voice of my father, his brute voice now a gasping, choking rasp. The stove shook and then a man wept. Impossible. My father never wept! A donkey pulled a cart past the window, the little bells on its neck fading as it retreated. Around the corner, children chanted in a sing-song rhythm, punctuated here and there by the bouncing of a ball. My head throbbed, as if the larvae of a fly was burrowing through my brain. My skin pulled away from me in an attempt to separate from my flesh and I was suddenly the mother, the threadbare fabric of the dress falling over me like iron shavings, beautiful and suffocating. I turned my head to listen to the children. Funny, I knew that song. The coffee boiled over, it was the colour of my mother. I tilted my head this way and that like a bird, looking for the music, but there was only the silence of the cupboard.

I returned with the black, thick liquid, a cardamom seed floating on top like a crocodile in wait. The girl sipped lightly. She kept her eyes on me. She pointed to a chair I hadn't noticed, and I collapsed on it gratefully, sighing to catch my breath.

I waited for her next request.

RAMADAN

She works the flour with water and sprinkles of salt. Into the middle goes an egg. Sinking her fingers into its cold stickiness, she rolls the palm of her hand to this side and that. Shoulders push down from the hip, lips creasing in small lines the harder she pushes and the faster she rolls and the deeper she rocks. Rolling, flattening and dividing into smaller balls. Some knotted, some pressed into rows, some dunked in sugar and nuts, some thrown over the balcony to the dogs.

No time to watch the oven, no time to check the clock, but the TV is on. Her back to the screen, she is rolling and pushing and heaving the dough and the dogs are groaning go, go, go. She doesn't count the cookies but they fill the trays and she covers them with damp towels, damp shirts, damp shorts, damp socks. Draining the teacup, she lingers on the sugar, sucking the waterlogged mint leaves between her teeth.

Now and then her eyes are wide open. She passes the TV on the way to the balcony. Leans over to shake the rope to see that the basket is secure. Inside, the television casts its blue reflection on her face but her ears stay outside and she hears the clip of donkey hooves and the scrape of wooden wheels and the cries of the man who will fill up her basket. She runs back out and waves. She lowers him some cookies. He loads tomatoes to squeeze, lettuce to break, onions to slice, and potatoes to clean. She will pay him tomorrow.

The rope is old but it never tears and she pulls it up, puts the food in the sink, turns on the cold water which in the summer is always hot.

The television is close by. Close to her back, to the bowls of cookies, close and closer. There are fat and happy cows dancing with their udders in the air and she listens to the song and opens the fridge, letting the cool cold air blow her back out to the balcony. *"Ya Walid!"* A boy on the crossways crisscross street stops when he hears her voice.

He takes a handful of coins from the basket and skips in a zig to the little store on the corner, walks in a zag back to the balcony, puts a bottle of milk into the basket. She gives him a cookie. He asks for another.

The music on the television makes her belly ripple and sometimes she twirls a hand in the air to dance with the flies. The voice of the woman brings tears to her eyes. The voice, that voice, meeting the night, her voice steeping like leaves in hot water. *Aqbal il-leil.* The sun glares off the screen, the afternoon wind pushing the curtains into clouds that billow against her back. Three dozen cookies come out of the oven all at once and three dozen more slide right back in. Her doughy arms waft into the air, throwing shadows of flour smudges onto her cheeks. The dogs have come again to turn in circles under the balcony. The street begins to squeal with children in their dusty green uniforms. She throws some cookies out over the railing and heaves her body back to work.

She doesn't have an iron and her clothes keep wrinkling. Under her arms and down her back and at the folds of her belly the fabric meets and gathers into streaks of the day's work. She washes her dress. From under the beds and behind the couch and in the corners she hunts for all the dirty clothes. She scrubs, pounds and bends over them like they were dough balls. She pulls and tears at them as if she were to tear them apart. At the edge of the tub, she kneels. Wet legs, wet arms, wet shoulders, wet red fingers deep in the creases of fabric, lost in the humid dirt, probing through traces of flour and cookies and dogs and spit and fraying rope.

She straightens her back and shuffles to the balcony. The street is coming and going and tossing itself up to her feet in handfuls of dust and dried leaves. She shakes out the wet clothes, her hands gripping the corners of each piece, shaking, flapping them into her legs, beating mountains into flat plains.

Shirts and pants and dresses hang over the line, shrinking in the dry air.

The afternoon is almost over. She falls to her knees again and again, lips moving silently, eyelids fluttering, fingers shaking. In her prayers she sings those words. That voice, that voice, that voice. She rides up to the night on a horse's back tasting the lips of the lover. This is how she always prays. She tells no one.

Her husband comes home and he eats her food, her children come home and they eat her food. The fasting has imploded with the sound of the gun, with the music on the television, with the banging of fists in rice. The hunger, the hunger. She hears that voice again. She rides a caramel horse sweet as the moon. The television is on while she washes dishes. Her husband yells out the jokes she has missed and her children yell out to each other.

She dries her hands on her lap, smokes a cigarette, eyes dropping, mouth relaxing. The TV is telling stories that she knows aren't true so she falls asleep to a horse, a horse. Later, her children are tired and her husband is tired so she wakes up to fold out the mattresses on the floor. She eats more food. The food is cold to her dark lips. She brings in the clothes and folds them into piles like stale bread and lets her eyes droop and mouth relax and head fall on a pile of sheets and there she sleeps.

WINTER, WATER, THE WAITER

Winters in a hot country are deceiving. A gentle morning sky entices a Canadian family out of their hotel and onto the busy streets. All around them the locals are wrapped in sweaters and scarves. Are they crazy, the tourists wonder, it's so hot!

It is Saturday and the family visits the Egyptian Museum, Coptic Cairo, and Khan el Khalili. They are careful to never pay more than the "average Egyptian," so they haggle and bargain at every turn. The leather bag from Luxor had cost ten pounds and the shawl from Siwi only four. Emboldened, they take it up with the taxi driver who has been ferrying them all day. No native Egyptian would pay more than ten pounds for a cross-city trip, they tell each other. No working-six-days-a-week wearing-the-same-shoes-for-years and five-children-he-can-hardly-feed Egyptian would pay more, so why should they? Watch and learn, says the father. But the daughter and son catch the expression on the taxi driver's face and see that value and price are two different things. No matter.

The family eats their dinner at the Ramses Hilton. Waiters in black polyester tuxedos serve peasant food on porcelain plates. French fries extra. The sky darkens, a muezzin chants the Quran, the tourists write their postcards. *So noisy!* they scribble.

They ask about the Nile boats that serve drinks at night and promise a belly dancer or two. Now wouldn't that be a hoot. The waiter gives directions; advises that they bring their jackets before heading out after sunset. His English is good, they generously tell him. Please, he insists, it will get cold, especially on the water. The waiter's voice carries both authority and resignation. Glancing up, the girl sees a boy her age and a look of surprise crosses her face.

"Don't be silly," the mother says. "Do you know it's snowing where we come from!"

The father motions for the bill. Nudging his daughter, he clears his throat and addresses the waiter. "What say we knock off a few pounds from this total, eh? Drinks on the house?"

"Dad."

"Nick," murmurs his wife. "This is a five-star hotel, they don't do that here."

"Oh come on, of course they do." He stares brightly at the young man.

The waiter shifts awkwardly. "You can pay me or pay at the desk," he says.

"Dad, let's just go," says the girl. It is not clear what she finds more mortifying: appearing poor or causing a scene.

"No, no. This is normal for them, watch." He looks up at the waiter and speaks in a tone he must imagine is both persuasive and charming. "We ate a lot here, *yalla yalla*. Good food, good food, the best. What do you say we just throw in the desserts. Delicious, yes? Do we need to speak to the manager?"

"*Dad*." The girl hits her father in the ribs. Now she must want to give the boy *all* their money. She and the waiter make eye contact and she sees that he is upset. For a brief moment, they share the universal language of adolescent embarrassment.

The mother gets up and opens her wallet. Credit card in hand, she walks over to the desk. The waiter follows, relief visible in the quickness of his steps.

Blue patio lanterns dangle along the riverbank, and the father wonders what holiday the Arabs are celebrating now. Traditionally dressed men escort them onto a boat deck where the vinyl seats shock their unsuspecting skin. They huddle together as close as is comfortable, which is not very close. The thick scarves and acrylic sweaters worn by a quartet of musicians remind them of their warmer clothes back at the hotel.

"But we're practically at the equator," complains the father.

"Not really," says the son to no one. "We're actually thousands of kilometres away."

Somewhere on the deck a tabla player begins with a dum-da-da-dum-da, then a violinist and clarinetist pick up the rhythm. Like a wave rolling in, an oud joins.

"Let's dance!" says the mother. She's going to enjoy this evening, it's decided. "To keep warm, come on!"

"Are you kidding me?" asks the daughter. Whatever excitement the trip held is now gone. If it's not this monument it's that museum, and everywhere in between is dust and noise, noise and dust. All of it in the company of her dopey parents and oblivious brother. She drinks a hot *sahlab*, grimacing with every sip. "This is disgusting."

The waiter looks her way and motions to the busboy to bring a mint tea instead. She passes back the sweet starchy drink without looking up. "Well that was horrible."

Winters in a hot country mean the waiter can afford meat for Fridays. Fresh lamb carcasses hang in the awning of a butcher's shop. Carved directly off the animal, wrapped in newsprint, the meat is warm and comforting, bought with his Thursday wages. The Nile flows softly beside him almost the entire way home. He crosses the Corniche at Imbaba, the old camel market and poorest neighbourhood in the city.

He sinks the meat in yogurt, cumin, and salt and then goes to sleep. The next morning, he arranges himself on his bed with a pad of paper on his lap, and writes. In between writing he prays. He doesn't work until Saturday afternoon, first the hotel then the boat, so he cooks the mid-day meal as his mother ensures he is not bothered. Her son writes and the Quran is written; she recognizes the sacred even if she can't read it. The meat simmers in the pan as he mixes words in his head. He spreads newspaper on the floor and lays out plates of stew and rice. He calls his mother, his three sisters, and his brother to sit and eat. There is much chatter but he finishes quickly. Back in his notebook, he has shaped a delicate contour with his pen and filled in flesh with consonants. It waits for him.

The next morning he returns to the centre of the city, passing packs of dogs and barefoot children as he traces his steps along the river bank. The surface of the water undulates, a heave from a boat, a ripple from a fish. The furrows remind him of the ever-changing shape of letters and he wonders if the Arabic language was born from this shape-shifting river. The way an adrift baby became Moses, Arabic letters change their form depending on their place in the word. In the world.

It is a short walk from the hotel to the boat, its lights glowing in the early night, and the waiter changes into a crimson galabaya and a Turkish fez, another costume for tourists. Tray in hand, he approaches a table. He has been waiting on foreigners for over a year and still he is surprised by their smiles. They are never happy, even when they are happy. At the end of the evening, Adil will roll some bills into his hand. Happiness is beside the point.

A girl his age slouches over the railing while the rest are dancing. Her mother pulls at her but is slapped back. The waiter waits for the mother's reaction, but there is none. The girl finishes her tea and throws her gold-encrusted glass into the water.

The waiter and the busboy exchange glances. Someone is going to have to pay for that glass. The busboy decides it won't be him and turns on his heels into the kitchen. The waiter leans over the side but the glass is gone. The girl frowns at him.

"It wasn't a person, just a glass," she scoffs.

He is uncomfortable when foreigners look at him; he knows what they see. *Native Egyptian with fez!* But there is a stillness in her eyes that is also calming, curious even. Then he remembers: she is the girl from the hotel restaurant at dinner. She mutters something that he doesn't quite catch. She extends her hand. A shy flutter stirs inside his chest.

"Can I try on your hat?"

"Sorry?"

She speaks up. "That's really a crazy hat. Can I try it on?"

He steps back, reaches up to his head. "No, no, sorry. No." If Adil sees, he will send him to the kitchen, away from the tourists—and the tips. He is disheartened, maybe she's been drinking. That's what tourists do, get drunk. How else to explain the crystalline voices, the impersonal slaps on the back, the laughter that exits their throats like torpedoes.

The girl hesitates, as if she understands she has come on too strong, said the wrong thing, maybe even pushed him away. But aside from English the only other language she speaks is bravado, like her father, and guile, like her mother. This is the best she can do with her limited skills.

"Do you always wear it or is it just for work because sometimes I see people wearing them and sometimes I don't. Like, it's hard to tell what's put on for tourists and what's real. How're you supposed to know what's fake? Why are we even here? Have you ever been to Canada? Ha, well if you come make sure it isn't January, that's for sure." She exhales noisily and rolls her eyes.

The waiter doesn't know if he understood everything. What does she want with his fez? He searches through his English vocabulary, but not one word for what he wants to say. Adil is suddenly behind him, "*Yalla ya homar.*" As if calling him a donkey is not enough, he slaps the boy on the back of the neck. As his eyes liquify, the girl looks at him with unexpected warmth. Adil yells again. The waiter jumps and runs to the other end of the boat where a quiet group from Italy are watching a felucca passing off the stern. Inside it, a small propane light flickers in the darkness as a man and woman cook the day's catch. The waiter hovers over the tables, picks up empty glasses, replaces napkins, wipes spills, calms down.

But a sudden yelp bursts through the air and even the music stops. The busboy and Adil begin screaming at each other. Adil looks strange, different, though the waiter can't quite figure out why. The girl's father is yelling at everyone, the mother is yelling at the father.

But where is she? Alarmed, the waiter runs to the railing and leans over. Something floats in the darkness and in one stroke he pulls the galabaya up over his head. He puts his right foot on the railing and is about to heave himself over when he is yanked back. Adil kicks him for good measure.

"Son of a dog! Do you want to increase my humiliation?"

"But the girl!"

Just then, a husk of laughter pierces the commotion. He can't figure out where she is but she is clearly not overboard.

"I didn't do it on purpose!" she protests. "It just flew away, there was a gust of wind." The mother slaps her arm. The father stands with his hand to his forehead, muttering. The brother smirks.

The waiter looks out on the water. A fez floats jauntily on the surface and he realizes why Adil looked odd. In a collective collapse, the family retreats to their benches. The girl catches the waiter's eye and shrugs conspiratorially. She leans over her brother and peers into the water. "It looked stupid on him anyways, plus he hit our waiter." Her father yanks her back into her seat.

"No more dancing," Adil says to everyone. He calls the waiter. "You. In the kitchen. Enough out here."

"But...Please. I need my tips."

Adil tsks in the universal Arabic signal for *don't bother me anymore.*

The waiter refuses to beg, but the injustice is too much. He knows how the night will end. Her parents will tuck a generous wad of dollars into Adil's hand and say something about sunstroke, and that money will go right into Adil's pocket. The busboy snickers and throws the waiter a towel. He spends the rest of the trip drying glasses.

The boat docks with a bump. The waiter puts his galabaya back on, replaces his fez, and leaves the kitchen to stand with the rest of the staff. Her family are the last to disembark, hands gingerly holding the velvet rope that leads to shore. He imagines the parents have already given Adil enough money to not only replace his fez but pay for his son's education. Bitterness grips him. But just as the girl disembarks, she runs back and, smiling—kindly? unkindly? he cannot tell—presses something into his hands. Then she tears off down the gangplank and is lost in the commotion of the busy Corniche. Suppressing a smile, he puts it directly in his pocket. It feels like money.

The walk home is long and the waiter is more tired than usual. He keeps one hand in his pocket around the dollar bills. He thinks ahead to his mother's reaction, to his siblings clamouring for gifts, to the fountain pen he saw on Talat Harb street. The bowab is asleep at the entrance of the building. He climbs the stairs and, before entering the small flat, decides to pull the folded paper containing money out of his pocket before showing his mother. He unfolds it slowly so that when he sees it is only the boat's menu, his heart stops with disbelief. But just before he tears it to pieces, he notices handwriting.

the night is too big for—it begins. He is astonished: it is a poem.

small things: a glass, a fez, your face
long rivers, the waiter, my tea
this stupid girl acting drunkenly
when all I drank was the night
but it was too big for me

After rereading the poem a dozen times, he folds the paper and puts it in his pocket. He goes back downstairs and sits on the front step of his building, quietly so the bowab doesn't wake. The moon fills up the sky while the clouds slice past, shredding it into small pieces. He fishes for a pen in his pocket, turns the menu around to find a blank spot, and begins to write.

A THOUSAND AND ONE NIGHTS IN PALMYRA'S BED

Queen Zenobia rose from the Euphrates enrobed in hot oils, perfume and salt. The enemy loomed beyond a mirage of smoke and glistening spears. For twelve more than twenty months, her armies kept watch in formation inside the thick stone walls of their fortress city. She was commander of the fiercest generals as they withstood occupation and empires and the Roman siege of Palmyra. They made promises to themselves and to each other.

Seeming like me. Looking, talking, feeling, touching just like me. Turning my head when he called: Noha. Another story broken. Noha.

My mother heard me close the heavy door.

"Hungry?" she asked, kissing my cheeks. I told her that it was hot outside, that I was hot, that the house was hot.

"What are you cooking, Mama?"

"You'll like it," she smiled.

The letter had arrived on the dot. The mailman was annoying but predictable, holding it up to the light as I ran towards him. "A letter from Ali!" he had said, like he always did. I grabbed it from his slippery hands. I shoved it into my shirt as Mama called, working hard to keep the corners of the envelope from jutting out. But she only watched my face as I ate.

"Thanks, Mama." It was so good.

"Noha." She looked out the window. "Do you think we should try and phone Ali again? It's been months since he wrote and I'm getting worried."

I folded my arms over the stubby corners of my blouse. It was getting hotter; the house, the kitchen, my face. Someone had painted the walls green before I was born and now the colour had paled and was seeping onto our shoulders. We had become the colour of walls, much paler and more translucent than Ali's absence.

"He's just working hard, Mama. Don't worry about it."

"It's not right that your brother doesn't write to us more often."

"He's very busy!"

"I am going to talk to Uncle about it. He will have some influence with him."

"What for? We'll go to the Centrale tomorrow and phone him, okay? Ali's been away so long I don't think he notices a few months anymore."

I put his letter with the others. A thick and wrinkled pile underneath socks and pens and undershirts. Almost five years' worth of letters and I managed to intercept nearly all of them, letting only a few through, the ones that said nothing; the difference between strategy and recklessness. I wanted him erased, I wanted Mama to anticipate the worst, I wanted his return to be unimaginable. The corners of this room were yellow. Ali's picture hangs next to Papa's. A slow crack ran out from underneath the frames to a spot above my bed. You look so much like Papa, Ali. But when Papa smiled I was not afraid. I remembered Ali's lips moving and his hands bending my legs into the tight spaces where he hid me. His engineering skills even then on display.

"Dear Ali, Mama sends you her love, Uncle too..." I sat on my bed and wrote. We have not forgotten the sound of your voice, Ali, how it broke everything, not just the silence.

I continued the letter. "We await your arrival anxiously. Your room is made up. Mama fills it with fresh flowers every day. I will be finished my exams by the time you arrive and we can all go to Alexandria together."

Then I lay in wait for my thoughts. The shutters were pulled tight and green smoke perfumed the mosquitoes to dust. Mama made tea one more time while an orchestra of television sets clanged outside the walls of our small flat. Later, the heavy bodies in dark rooms around us began to break with sleep, we heard their every rumble. When will Ali come home? How much shorter can the days get? How much longer is the space between my shadow and my sleep? The night is like a thin knife sliding down my hip. I must grab its hilt before—

Rome wanted what belonged to Rome. Palmyra's soldiers sharpened their arrows and gripped their spears, emptying the air of everything but anticipation. All night long, they held their breath. War was inevitable. No one slept.

He will walk into the house like an Ottoman governor. I will become a crack in the wall that must be plastered over. Mama and I will be reupholstered and shuffled about in new but suffocating patterns. He will sit on us and cross his legs and spill his tea. I am young and unmarried and Ali will see to it that I remain neither.

I was twenty and he was thirty and I had always seen both my past and future in his eyes. My life was compressed to a few spaceless, timeless points, casting no shadows, uttering no sounds. He would find me an ashen husband, an old one, a wet man oozing onto his job and then, afterwards, oozing onto me. Mama would dress my hair and my body and at night, when she thought I was asleep, she would cry and drink her tea.

The people did not understand about waiting. Waiting behind walls, weapons at the ready. Waiting at dusk for dawn and waiting at dawn for their queen to appear. She was in the tent for days until one morning broke differently. There was a rumble of men and a screeching of horses. Queen Zenobia was born holding a sword and that was how she would die, she vowed, charging ahead of them all. There was no time for prayer.

So here I am, the bathroom is draining a layer of myself to some distant land. I keep my eyes on the water as two hands cover me in a towel that drapes to the floor. I am carried to a bed that is soft that is big that is dark and deep and I am told I am loved between breaths that rise in tremors and pitches. My body is two hands that aren't mine. My face is the kisses of sunken ships. My legs convulse like a disease. I am not spared the blade but I survive the thrust. This is how a story should be told.

"Noha! Quickly, get ready. What are you doing still in bed?" Mama opened the shutters, blinding me. "Get up child, I don't want us to be late."

"What time is it?"

Mama sat on my bed, looking tired and forgotten. She searched for my feet from outside the blankets, absentmindedly squeezing at the folds and bumps as if I were already just a memory. "Late, almost five. You take such long naps, child. Get up and have something to eat."

"Can't we take a taxi?"

"The bus is good enough. I want you to wrap the gift and sign the card."

"What's his name again?"

"They are calling him Yahia. Get up, Noha, it's not every day your cousin has a baby-naming ceremony."

I had a dress that I bought the year before and had rarely worn. It was green and modest, making me look younger. I did not like it, but it was how I must look for the family. Mama and I took two buses to the Tenth of Ramadan City, an atrocious suburb between Cairo and the desert. Elham and Mounir had boasted endlessly about the services available in the neighbourhood and the spaciousness of their new apartment. I thought they had been banished to a faceless mirage. By the time we arrived at their door, I was already weary of the feast.

But Mounir swept us inside to a haze of smoke and sugar. He was dull but sweet, always winking at everyone. He pulled me to the corner as he took my jacket. "How are prospects, Noha? I am dying to see you married!" His breath smelled of cheap cigarettes, and the darkened bump on his forehead attested to the fervour with which he performed his prayers. But I imagined him hitting his head against the refrigerator instead, encouraging the bruise. Elham, my cousin, the woman he had consigned to mediocrity, rescued me.

"Come Noha, come see Yahia." She took me into the bedroom where layers of white lace formed an ascending spiral over the infant's crib. He was too small to be believable, so I looked for him in his mother's eyes. Elham kissed his mouth then smiled at me. The hush between us reminded me of when we were younger, passing hours and hours together never saying a word, trying to divine what the other was thinking and feeling. But she broke the spell. "Is the good news true, Noha?"

"What good news?"

"That Ali is coming back from the Gulf, finally?"

"What? How—when did you hear that?"

"Well, you know that he and Papa are always in touch because of Papa's business. Why didn't you tell us that Ali is coming home, and with a fiancée no less! Are you and your mother keeping secrets from us?"

The baby started to cry and in the wailing I could barely hear the shattering of my chest. I hurried from the bedroom and in the far corner of the salon, beyond plates and plates of food, found Mama and Uncle. If Uncle has told her what he knows, then it is already too late. My feet stumbled on a landslide and carried me there. "Mama, I must talk to you."

"Noha, where are your manners? Kiss your Uncle." He stood up, elegant and kind, looking directly into my eyes. I liked him and the kiss I planted on his cheek was sincere.

"Mama, can you come, please? I have to talk to you." Mama looked at her brother-in-law then back at me. Quizzically, she followed me to a private spot in the hallway.

"I have to go, Mama, we have to go. Now."

"Noha, what are you talking about?"

"I'm sick, I don't feel well. Can we go, please, now?"

"What is the matter?"

"I just don't feel well, it's that time, Mama, I have to go home." Her eyes dropped to the lower half of my dress, searching for clues of blood or warring tribes.

"Noha, why do you never prepare yourself? Maybe if you spoke to Elham, or somebody else?"

"No Mama! I have to go, I feel sick. I'm going to faint, I'm going to throw up." I wasn't lying this time. The floor rose to meet the wall behind me, sucking me into the vortex. I was getting pale, my brow was burning, I clutched at my belly.

"This is terrible, how embarrassing." Mama grabbed my arm and took me to the door. "Put on your coat and I will say goodbye to everyone."

Zenobia, ruler of Palmyra, empress of the Aramaeans, Queen of the Syria Phoenice. Her name made the Romans shake with anger, made them think twice, wrenched them from their moorings. Her greatness was a challenge to their own. She mocked them with her cities of culture and learning, her men of great dignity, her women of impeccable honour. The Romans had ridden for weeks to set up camp outside her gates. She had patience, but they had numbers. They called out to her one last time.

I am no queen, but—"Do you like it?" He is a thief, a traitor, the executioner. "Do you like this?" His voice crests around the dry hollow it opens. "Do you like this?" It spins like a lost ship through the cold, wave after wave, sinking down with the undertow. I turn to salt when Ali looks at me. Time is curled under my tongue, dissolving my gut, burning the insides of my ribs. I anticipate the soft sticking flesh of his insistence. I twist myself around and around, turn my spine into teeth, my hair into snakes, my feet into crumbling bridges. Ali's shadow obliterates the sky. I will not let him back into this house. There will be battle.

I sat squished in the back seat of the car with Mama, Tanta Samira, Elham and Yahia. Uncle drove and Mounir smoked endless cigarettes, choking us all. My green dress grew darker under the armpits and every time Mounir looked back I had to tug it again below my knees. I kept my eyes fixed ahead, trying to match my swerves with the road's swerves, my nausea with the noxious fumes and stenches of the city. Many times a lump rose in my throat, many times I swallowed it. I swore I would not say a word.

The airport was overrun with families meeting the incoming plane. I wanted to trip over the luggage ramp and fall forever into oblivion. Saudi men and women disembarked first, already looking over our heads and into the Mercedes limousines that awaited them. Then the Egyptians emerged, returning home from their working exile, dancing into our midst. Tears and wails and clapping greeted them and they swooned like wounded soldiers. Ali parted the current when he saw our faces and ran towards us. Behind him, almost forgotten, his fiancée, barely older than I, was engulfed by her own family. Ali kissed us all and we pulled him towards the car. He laughed and strutted and threw us gifts. To me, he bent down and said, "Noha, *ya asal,* the biggest gift for you." Then a wink and a shout, "The biggest wedding Cairo has ever seen!" Mama cried and hugged her son even more.

Ali was rich. He had become a prince, a king, a ruler of his world, he told us. His years working for the American dollar and the Saudi riyal meant that no door could close for him again, no sky could darken without his permission, no mother, no sister, could deceive his expectations or threaten his status. His hands swept the stuffy rooms of our home and pointed to furniture and belongings that *must go.* In their place he would order only the finest Italian furniture, the most efficient Swedish appliances. He slapped the walls and announced the new colours they would become. He sat Mama down and told her that never again would she have to clean or cook or sew. That from now on she would live in luxury. He told us stories of the Gulf, of the many people he had befriended from all over the world, of the adventures and exciting moments he had experienced, of the mountains of money he'd let us peek at if we were good. Mama fell asleep in the chair long before Ali was finished, so he continued his remembering for my sake, even opening a bottle of American whiskey when he knew she was still for the night. His fiancée, Shireen, he told me, was from a very good family. They had been living in Riyadh for the last five years while her father taught at the university. Now they were all returning home.

"She has two brothers, you know. And many cousins! I want you to meet them all, and choose one for your husband. Then our families will be welded together forever," he said greedily. "Shireen does not go to university and I don't think there's any point in you continuing. Now, don't argue, you know Papa would say the same thing. It's only because I have been away so long that you have lost guidance and direction."

Papa would not have said the same thing. Ali's words began to crash and swerve into each other as I followed him out onto the balcony. The swift evening air refreshed him, and he waved to the stars, singing the words to a French song he could barely remember. Beneath him the city roared in approval. He jumped up on a chair and, bottle in hand, composed an ode to the richness of life. The air was thin and yielding, everything was yielding for Ali. He dug in his pockets and pulled out a handful of coins, tossing them over the side. We both looked over to watch them fall. He laughed, "You see, Noha, we are so far up we can't even hear them crash to nothingness. Some poor beggar will pick them up in the morning and thank Allah for his generosity." He laughed uproariously at this. "And I thank Allah for his generosity to *me*. And you, little sister," in a sweeping gesture, "may thank *me* for my generosity to *you*."

His mouth bubbled like wet bread. He bent low and brushed his face against mine, whispering something unfamiliar like my name. *Noha. Noha.* He stood tall again and tossed more Saudi coins over the side of the balcony. Propped high on the chair like that, with the railing only reaching to his knees, he was like a wild dog jumping from car to car. His arms, tanned and proud, gestured rhythmically to the lights below, his strong legs balancing the chair beneath him, its one shorter leg keeping him dancing. My eyes caught the space between his thighs and his hips and I saw him rise like a coral-encrusted ship from the depths of the sea bottom. He saw me watch him. His lips trembled and his eyes hesitated only a second before dilating and fixing their gaze on my body.

"Noha, you are so pretty. Look how pretty you have gotten."

Both his hands reached toward me, but I stepped back.

He lifted one foot to step down, but the chair moved in the opposite direction and he had to concentrate hard to keep it steady. He let the empty bottle slide from his hands to the concrete floor of the balcony. Its smithering crash was barely noticed by either of us. We both claimed the chair with our eyes. He mumbled, "Could you just grab it for me please? Steady it."

He struggled to keep his balance. I rested my foot against one of the legs, in an effort to calm it, maybe, but every time he lowered his foot to descend, it threatened to tip backward. He swayed above me, trying to steer clear of the railing.

"Noha, what are you doing? I'm going to fall."

He said those words in a drunken laugh at the absurdity of the thought. Ali fall? The great and powerful Ali? Fall?

Our eyes met with an abrupt shock, the hard edges of our thoughts stopping all at once and converging at a point of frightening understanding. He frowned. Then he looked almost sad. When it rose up again in the slippery see-sawing of his balancing act, I slipped the toe of my foot under the shorter leg of the chair. Our gazes remained locked on each other as his body was suspended in a parenthesis of an embrace. His hands were inches from my shoulders.

Then, with all my strength, I kicked my foot up and heaved the chair over with a grand cry.

Ali arced over backwards. I imagined he could see the horizon upside-down. His trousers tugged at the railing, then his ankles. One of his slippers came off and landed at my feet. His body swooped like a leaf caught in an updraft then, as if being sucked from below, vanished from my sight. I looked over the edge, but, of course, I was so far up that I couldn't hear him crash to nothingness.

The Romans promised death and turned it into sand. They laid siege, set fire to the fields and ramparts, starved the people, ambushed soldiers by the thousands, massacred children, raped women, beheaded the bravest of men. The unimaginable became Palmyra's legacy. And the mightiest Zenobia, Queen of Palmyra, was paraded through the city like a caught lion, her name obliterated, her lands overrun by the careless and the compromised, later to be entombed and forgotten in a barren desert. She vowed revenge and buried her heavy tears in the city's dirt. How had it come to this?

And yet, and yet, and yet.

Mama, it's me, Noha. I am in Palmyra's bed, armour still glistening from yesterday's battle. A voice whispers in the breeze and touches my face. What are you saying to me, Queen Zenobia, in your language of stone and steel? If I walked among your relics, would I hear you proclaim this land a nation? Would you shake off your occupation like I have shaken off mine? I have filled my heart with your ambitions. Don't worry that we have lost: the Romans lie in ruins too. Palmyra, listen to me. We are alive.

HAMDO THE HERO

Sometimes Hamdo understood fame. Let others have the paparazzi and fur coats and fancy cars, or even drugs and whoredom and death—like that *sharmouta* Marilyn Monroe—he had something none of these clowns had. He had the respect of his wife and kids and everywhere he went the neighbours saluted and the cashier girls imagined he was their lover. Everywhere he went people applauded. He was a handsome sheikh and they asked each other, who is that man, that man who escaped, who crossed the ocean, who is that hero? Who is that Hero Hamdo?

Hamdo drove a cream-coloured Mercury Monarch—the carriage of kings!—and when it pulled into his driveway every day at 5:30, the curtains in the living room window shook.

But Marvin was standing there with his stupid little dog.

"Hello Harry," Marvin stuttered.

Hamdo flinched at the name. He hated Marvin for drawing it out, as if the man knew it was a film of suffocating plastic over his amber skin. This called out for a flexing of muscle.

"Hello Marvin," he said, stepping out of the car. "How's your love life?" Hamdo winked. Marvin must know that his wife was the unsightliest woman on the block, with her shortened leg and thick neck and one side of her mouth frozen on never-said words.

Hamdo moved his head back and forth in a little conspiratorial dance. "Let me know if you need any pointers." He added with an affected stage whisper, "Or girlfriends." He walked away in time to miss Marvin's dog shitting on Harry's grass, and it staying there. He walked away needing to wash the name Harry off his skin with the same industrial soap he used to scrub his hands after work.

The two youngest were playing in the living room, blocks and puzzle pieces spread out over the thin brown carpet. The two older ones were at the kitchen table, books open. "Hi Daddy." They reminded him of his sisters, their reed-like voices hanging in the air like aftershocks.

"Where's Mommy?" he asked. No one answered. "Where's Mommy?" he asked again. The kids looked at each other. He slapped the table hard. The kids jumped. The youngest one's face rippled and he started to cry.

"Where's your mother?" Hamdo's voice boomed like a fighter jet. The eyes of his children were wide, innocent, in awe of his dominance, like he must have been when he saw the soldiers. It made his heart bloat with an indecent pride and his veins swell with power.

"I'm here."

She entered the living room carrying a basket of laundry, hair falling unceremoniously around her face, She was wearing those slacks, the ones that pulled up way too high and made her look fat. "You've been eating all day," he said, grinning wide so she could see all his teeth. She looked away and managed a smile, the eyes of the children on her every move. She sat down on the couch and pulled out the pieces one by one, folded them, set them in neat piles. He went down the hall to clean and change. Water ran hard and drawers slammed loudly in the now-silent house.

He came out singing a familiar song. "Who's the hero Hamdo, who's the hero Hamdo man? Who's the hero Hamdo, who's the hero Hamdo man?"

He flexed his arms and caressed his biceps. Lucky kids! To have such a strong and impressive father. Not like his own Baba, not weak in the presence of authority. Not flinching in the face of annihilation. Not in pieces and clumps because he believed what they said about him.

"Feel this," he said. "Feel this!"

They kept their eyes on the blocks and on their books. "Come on!" he yelled. He danced around the table, round and round. "Who's the hero Hamdo, who's the hero Hamdo man? Who's the hero Hamdo, who's the hero Hamdo man?" His wife stood up and he grabbed her rear end. She was seated next time he went around the living room.

Finally, the youngest one succumbed. He leapt for his father's strong arm like a monkey. Hamdo hoisted the little boy up as high as he could. "Yalla!" he said. "Yalla!" He grabbed the child's waist and held him aloft. "Now you can climb the ceiling!"

The little boy crawled like an upside-down spider. He giggled and laughed and called to his sisters. "Look at me!"

"Now let me fly," the boy said. "Now I want to be a hawk. A beautiful hawk!"

"A mighty hawk!" Hamdo corrected him. "Fly! Fly!" He turned the boy around and whooshed him through the air. He held him like a rocket and zoomed him around the girls and the mother, almost crashing into them each time.

"Hamid, you're being a little rough," his wife said quietly, untangling the boy's hands from her hair.

"Shut up," Hamdo said. His entire body was a weapon, click click, crack crack crack. Stay clear of the hero.

"Fly some more," the boy said. "Let go and let me fly. Like a hawk! Like a rocket!"

Hamdo stopped whooshing the boy for a beat and looked at him, his eyes squinting darkly. "Like a rocket? Are you sure? Are you sure you want to explode? You want me to let go of you?"

The boy threw back his head and giggled. "A rocket to the moon!"

"Hamid." His wife stopped folding laundry.

The oldest girl pushed back her chair and stood up. "Daddy," she said, her body bracing for a smack, only a slight quivering in her chin betraying her courage.

She will hate me, he suddenly thought. *She will hate me.*

"What?" he turned around sharply. "What? We're playing. I'm playing with my son."

"Daddy! Daddy! I want to fly! Caw caw!" The boy stretched out his tiny thin limbs and clouds parted for him, the sky was open and vast and warm. His father rocked and pumped him back and forth. The boy would cross the ocean and save himself just like he did, to hell with his sisters. "Are you ready, bird? One!" Back and forth again. "Are you ready, rocket? Two!"

"Hamid, don't you dare!"

"Three!"

The boy closed his eyes and stretched his arms out miles apart. His powerful wings took him above the clouds and circled over the forest. He was the most majestic of birds. In the brief second that his body soared through the air he heard the screaming call of his mother hawk. Then his face crashed into the wall. The rocket had torn a hole through the windows, the walls, the bedroom. It left him for dead.

"No!" The boy's mother wailed and jumped.

She landed on the child and folded his crumpled body into her arms. A streak of blood had followed him down the wall. It took him one second to fill his lungs again and when he did, he arched his back against his mother and howled. He kicked and grabbed at her, as if willing his broken hawk spirit to transfer into her resilient body, that she in turn might kick and grab and kill for him. Might kill *him*. But she only held the boy and cried, each of them cowering in the man's shadow. Blood poured out of the boy's mouth from where his tooth had been. He cried and coughed, cried and choked, cried.

"Stupid boy," Hamdo said, pacing. "Stupid boy." He poked at him with his foot. "Come on, I just did what you asked, you wanted to fly." Then he flinched involuntarily, it was his own tiny body crumpled on the stone floor, the room around him reduced to steel rods and concrete shards, a severed foot still wearing her slipper.

He turned around to see his daughters staring at him, the smallest one crying, the two oldest unable to conceal the contempt in their eyes. *They will hate me*. "What?" he shouted. "What!" He leaned over his wife and son. "Shut up, you two! And stop crying like a little girl. Who cares about that tooth, it was going to come out anyways. Who cares? Who cares?"

He pulled the boy up to his feet, but the fury in the child was still alive and he flailed at his father, all windmilling arms and legs, growling like a dog, shrieking like a raptor. Hamdo laughed. "Go to your mother," he said, tossing him onto his mother's lap. "You take care of your little girl," he added with disgust, and walked away. The boy buried his face in his mother's breast and sobbed.

Hamdo went downstairs to the basement. He had finished it with wood paneling last year so it looked like the basements he'd seen on American TV shows. He took pictures but had no one to send them to. He picked up a *Time* magazine from the stack on the table. "Peasants," he muttered to himself. "Peasants. *Idiots*. Staying for what. For what?"

He read the magazine and started to feel better. He was smart. He could read such things and not even in his own language. The magazine for intellectuals like him. World events at his fingertips! Who else from the old country was sitting in a Canadian bungalow reading *Time* magazine? *Wallah wahid*. Who else was brave enough to leave? They cannot resent him for escaping, for crawling out when he had the chance. They cannot! They had been imaginary people in a nonexistent land. To hell with it all. He obliterated their faces more and more each day. With every outburst, every meltdown, every explosion of anger. *Peasants*, he swore again.

They hate me.

Time passed, as it does, unknowable, unreachable, a beam of light casting no shadows, leaving no prints, its only purpose now to blast holes and cauterize wounds, the latter taking thousands of years. He smelled dinner cooking and realized he was famished. He sang as he climbed the stairs. "Who's the hero Hamdo, who's the hero Hamdo man? Who's the hero Hamdo, who's the hero Hamdo man?"

THE UGLY FATHER

An unremarkable man watches a little girl snake down a bright yellow slide. He's wearing dark green work pants, a khaki shirt, grey wool socks and cracked boots. He's the only adult not half-naked in the 30-degree heat.

The girl takes his hand and leads him over the sand. His staccato gait gives the impression that his knees can't bend farther than a few degrees. He pulls his cap down with a tug and doesn't look at anyone. Not the shiny fathers revelling in the multitude of maternal gazes. Not the tanning mothers sipping juice on the grass, upturned jaws and closed eyes mimicking serenity. Not the teenagers on the swings rocketing skyward and swearing loudly. He doesn't see the children scowling at their parents, screaming and swiping candies from each other, bawling when they trip. He doesn't notice the parents sighing, gritting their teeth, quickly assessing how hard they could yank an arm and get away with it. His thick hands dangle awkwardly, fingers looking for pockets to crawl into while his rough and pockmarked face hides under his cap like in a trench during wartime.

He looks at no one but his daughter. And she looks back at him.

"To the see-saw!" sings the little girl.

"Okay," he says, his voice so low that she is already in the habit of reading his lips.

He bends over it, not elegantly, and works it like a pump hauling water from a mine. That is to say, with expertise. She squeals, her dark hair flies up and her toes reach into the sky. He studies her, gauging when he could go faster and when he needs to ease up.

The sun is in his eyes and he squints, freeing a hand to jerk the cap down again. Each time she rises and silhouettes in front of him, images of her mother flicker against the sky. Had she ever looked at him like their daughter does now—freely, joyously, without grimacing? He struggles to remember.

But the girl totters as she eclipses the sun. A leg lifting too high sends her dangerously close to the edge. A grand terror ripples over her face like water.

"Daddy!"

Full of fear, he lets her drop like a piston, easing up at the last possible moment. She rolls off the seat with a giggle and runs to the swings, arms churning like paddles in whitewater, and jumps up and pumps her legs. He refrains from pushing until she has gotten herself to a height that matches his own. It is not such a great feat, but she doesn't know that yet.

They work in silence. She, her eyes closed against the wind. He, still as a tree trunk with an errant branch tapping at her back. Their shadows grow longer as the park begins to empty. He will bring the child back to the mother in an hour. They count the leaves on the closest tree.

"I counted ten thousand, fourteen hundred twenty-four sixty-seven two two two!"

"That's a lot of leaves."

"How many did you count, Daddy?"

"Oh, just half as much as that. You go too fast."

"It's because I get so close, Daddy. Look!" She swings up, helped by a stronger push than usual and points her toes deep into the branches, her laughter rustling with the starlings overhead. She throws her head back on the way down and lets her hair brush along the sand. Her upside-down eyes meet his and, in a moment both solemn and cavalier, she says, "I love you, Daddy."

"I love you too," he whispers.

She will grow up quickly, he thinks, and for the first time he cements a moment, this very one, and knows it will be the moment he will measure the rest of their lives against. Perhaps in just a few years he'll be picking her up after school, or she'll already be at the park, and she won't want to hold his hand or let him push her on the swing. She'll ask herself, he already knows, why he isn't charming like all the other fathers.

A year after that she'll be embarrassed by his wardrobe and the way he talks and the work he does—or doesn't. The year after that, the boys will be cute and the girls will be tough and she'll look at him from the bus stop and wish he was handsome or looked busy or smiled more.

The day will come, he feels himself getting sick now, that she will say to herself, *damn he's ugly.* And she will be embarrassed. Embarrassed to walk with him, embarrassed to introduce him to her friends, embarrassed that the flaws she sees in the mirror are the shortcomings he has bequeathed her.

This will go on for years. She will look away in a twitch of revulsion that he'll spot like a housefly detecting a moving hand. He will grow to fear their time together and harden his skin against it like a beetle's. She'll visit him grudgingly and roll her eyes constantly. And he'll be making her dinner, a bland affair of pasta and bottled sauce, when, between sips of her sweet coffee and rants about lost jobs and mean boyfriends, she'll empty the cup and scowl but then catch his eye for just a fraction, a tiny moment. A single instant. He'll be leaning heavily against the stove, stirring, nodding, saying yes, yes, yes. He will look up and it will seem to her that his eyes are upside down again, that what's left of his hair is brushing the sky between them as he swings above the sand. And it will dawn on her. It will crash like a tree full of leaves—and instead of running away from the startled birds like she always does, for once she'll dive right into them. And there it will be with the compost and the carrion: He loves her.

He doesn't care if her hair is dull, if her eyes aren't beautiful, if she is fat or plain or lonely. He doesn't care. And then she'll know, for the very first time in her life, that he is the only person who loves her like that. He is the only person in the entire universe who isn't judging, comparing, rejecting, calling her ugly.

She'll stop talking right then and there and look at him. Look right at him. The way she used to, he'll dare to think. And he won't speak. He'll put the spaghetti on her plate and they'll eat in silence and he'll notice that for once she isn't sighing or rolling her eyes or tapping her foot restlessly against the table. But once or twice she'll shake her head and laugh to herself, a soft laugh this time. When they're done, she'll pick up the plates and put them in the sink and before he can get up to wash them, she'll turn around.

"Wanna go to the park?" she'll ask.

And he won't say anything, won't even be able to breathe. She'll just take his hand and they'll put on their coats and go to the swings.

THE JOB

Day 1: I just got fired. My contract will not be renewed when it expires in two months because Boss-man does not want to renew it. Nothing specific, he said, just a question of fit. Said he wanted to open up the competition and see if he can get somebody better.

Day 2: Things I should have said: That there is always somebody "better." That it would have been nice to have a better manager. That I can point in any direction and land on someone who wished *he* was better. That firing a single mother doesn't make *anything* better. But instead I cried and more or less agreed with everything he said.

Day 3: I can't believe I have to work here for the next two months. He said I can "paint the picture" how I want, that if I want to tell people I am leaving of my own volition, he will not contradict it. Well, I have nothing to hide, if that's what he means. I tell everybody I was fired, enjoy their gasps of disbelief, and share in the catty comments that follow.

Day 4: I wonder if they are just being polite. Funny how nobody says, *But you were so good at your job.* Also funny how no one is keeping track of their pencils.

Day 8: Bob down the hall giving me hound-dog looks. Talk about a waste of space. And they fired *me*? Have decided I am going to keep myself and my daughter in pencils for the rest of our lives. A pencil a day for the next two months. Make that two pencils a day.

Day 9: It must have been shadowing me like a puppy how much I never liked this job. Do you know how many people don't like their jobs here? But I *really* did not like this job. Marketing. I cried the first two weeks out of frustration and boredom. Then I got used to it and tried to just go along. Then I got too used to it and stopped trying. Mia came home with a note from her teacher asking me to give her more pencils. This is a sign from the gods.

Day 12: Drag myself in quite late, hoping that he'll catch me and make some kind of comment, at which I can say *so fire me.*

Day 14: Took the day off.

Day 16: Bravado wears off easily. Still have to work. Wen doesn't make eye contact with me anymore. He's looking quite cocky in fact. I wonder if he has designs on my office. I have overestimated the number of pencils I can possibly live with. Time to start accumulating printer paper. Could I use a three-hole punch at home?

Day 19: Flippant remarks get you nowhere. Bossman and I in the elevator alone. Good God. It never happened before, but of course it has to happen now. I am in a good mood, having spent my entire morning filling out job applications. He asks, Will we see you at the national meetings next week? I say, oh I don't know, maybe. Well, not very flippant. Kind of mumbling.

Day 21: Printer paper is heavy when you're lugging packs of it home every night. Must have over three thousand sheets by now. I would take pens, but they only have ball points. Still a few weeks left in which to find a job. Am discovering that the following combination leads just about nowhere: liberal arts degree + years in the public sector + inability to work overtime or shifts due to family responsibilities. Bob came into my office this morning with a cup of coffee. He stared at me till I got off the phone then he said with a forced laugh: Coffee sure is hot this morning! Then he said: I always liked you, I'm going to be real sorry to see you go. I smothered a laugh, but he was dead serious. I prayed for the phone to ring and it did.

Day 22: Why do I even bother going to meetings? I find myself being extra attentive, asking pertinent questions, laughing like an American. Boss-man must be kicking himself for his misguided decision. Just how many paper clips can one use in the event of an apocalypse?

Day 23: I need my stapler but I took it home anyways. Must remember not to pilfer the essentials until the very end. I borrow Dina's stapler but before she hands it over, she writes her name on tape and sticks it on. Was up half the night imagining Boss-man meeting with Boss-woman, the two of them mournfully wondering how they can reverse the decision to fire me. I might not be the perfect fit, but I have so many special qualities, qualities they cannot afford to do without, they conclude. By the time I fall asleep they are making out.

Day 24: Did it! Managed to get a job interview for next week. One of the few jobs left in the world where having a robust social media presence is not a prerequisite.

Day 28: A reasonable presence on social media was a prerequisite. Jokes get you nowhere in job interviews. I said: Well, I was very social as a child. The woman squinted and the man cleared his throat. On to the next question: What unique qualities do you bring to this position? I said: Thrifted blazers and a pair of Fluevog shoes bought at their full price. Plus, I come with my own office supplies. In the bathroom after the interview I noticed that my glasses were completely crooked. I had forgotten that Mia scrunched them underfoot the night before.

Day 29: A polite call to say I did not get the job. I said: Oh thank you but I knew that already.

Day 32: Bob left a rose on my desk. And a note. He asked me to lunch. My first thought was why oh why does he have to be called Bob? With all the glorious not to mention manly names bouncing around, must I imagine myself with a Bob? I picture us dating: my hair cut in a bob, wearing bobby socks, we have to bob traffic, we feed our children apples bobbing in buckets of water. But he could be called Bruno and would I like him more? No.

Day 33: One must dodge traffic, not bob it. Bob took me to a Chinese buffet. Everything was sweet. Especially Bob. Especially when he told me he was married and a little bored. He said I was the kind of woman he had always fantasized about. I spent the rest of the meal seriously trying to figure out what it is about me that would elicit a man's fantasies. Nobody in their right mind would call me sexy. Still, flattery goes a long way. However, Bob is the most boring man I have ever shared a Chinese buffet with and that's not a category anyone wants to compete in. He told joke after joke. Jokes I'd seen on TikTok or worse, Facebook. I laughed at the first few and then started saying the punch lines before he got to them. He didn't find that funny.

Day 36: Another job interview looming on the horizon. Trying to keep my spirits up in spite of the fact that if ambition were a bone I'd be on crutches. Something like that.

Day 37: I can't believe it: Suzanne ordered two dozen gel pens, all in different colours. How is she able to justify gel pens as an essential office supply? I am impressed. She has clearly never been fired. The secretaries fawn over the pens. Managed to put four of them in my purse the minute she stepped out of her office. I love gel pens.

Day 40: Strange job interview. Felt detached from the whole process, which I think was a good thing. No stupid jokes, no giggly laughter, just me. It's only part-time, but pays enough that I could still pursue other endeavours such as effective housecleaning and in-situ shopping. Inventory currently accumulating under my desk: one French English dictionary, a 500-pack of assorted coloured paper, one box of Avery labels, substantial number of 5x7 notepads, two rulers, one three-hole punch, at least a dozen 100-gram packages of terrible coffee but what the hell, and a luxurious back-support cushion that was on Wen's chair but he is bugging me so much these days I just had to have it. He now has a permanently pained expression on his face.

Day 44: Got a call-back. They want me and another candidate to visit their office so we can get a better idea as to how it works there, and they will base their final decision on a whole host of things. Like how we manage the awkward placement of our hands while pretending to be casual, genuine and interested. On that alone, I will get fired all over again.

Day 46: Wasn't Moses in the desert this long? I spent my morning at the new office and remembered to gently smile at potential colleagues and nod my head when they explained the minutiae of tasks related to the post. But what I was thinking was this: I should have eaten breakfast and had another coffee.

Day 48: I got the job. This is too weird. I must have been possessed by a venture capitalist when I negotiated a higher salary. What I really wanted to ask was how flexible are they about the hours of nine and five? Can nine equal ten and can five equal four, all things being relative, all things being a single mom? The upside to all of this, if there is one, is that I start two weeks after I leave here. Which gives me a couple of weeks off. This place is going to crumble all around me in confusion, just you watch.

Day 49: Attention shoppers, the store is now closing! I added a beautiful brass lamp to my collection at lunch today. Everyone wants to know the gory details: where am I going (far), how much does it pay (tons), are there benefits (all the benefits), do I get holidays (weeks and weeks and weeks), is Boss-man upset (of course he is). Our entire interaction takes place via email now. He wished me luck in my future endeavours and used exclamation marks at the end of every sentence, and we all know that means he is suffering. Do I really need a blotter at home? Does anyone even know what a blotter is anymore? As a sort of unscientific experiment, I asked Bob where his blotter was. He didn't even answer.

Day 50: Even if it's not the kind of place I can sneak out of early, the new office is much closer to home and Mia's school than where I am now. None of this droning out on the highway—I can take my bike. I slept the entire night through last night and didn't dream of either foreclosures or streetwalking. Life is going to be good. The fear of firing, however, will always stay with me. Like an inoculation. Everybody should be fired at least once in their life, to ward against contagions such as laziness and ineptitude, laziness and insolence, laziness and laziness. There's no protection against petty thievery, however. I took Wen's iPad when everyone went outside for their afternoon smoke. Smoking is so bad for you.

HOW TO: YOUR VERY OWN LIFE

1. Budgeting: Curb your spending. At the entrance to the bank you see toes poking out of someone's boots as you stomp the snow off your own.

"Bonjour," an old man says, holding the door open. His other hand is stretched out for money.

The sky has just gone dark, and the kids are outside hitting the stop sign with chunks of ice (with instructions to yell if they see the bus coming) and now this guy wants your money. Except for the occasional toonie you save for the laundry, you rarely carry money. You're only there because kids need cash for their school bake sale. You pull your mitts off at the *guichet*, and two twenties flutter stupidly out of the slot. A glance at your balance makes your insides freeze. The old guy holds the door open as you leave. He tries to make eye contact, it's his best marketing technique, but you look down and barely mumble thanks. A group of teenagers come in to warm up. "Bonjour," he says. The girls snicker. You vow to give money to the next person who asks, but no one asks. When you find some coins a week later you feel rich.

2. Driving: Adjust your mirrors. A standard transmission is a thing of beauty. But you can't appreciate that. He yells at every gear shift so you miss out on the oily way it's supposed to move from second to third. You don't pay attention to how the engine coils around itself and, like a springtime crocus, comes to life. You hold your breath while the car crests the hill, the honking behind you competing with a noisy formation of geese overhead. They are returning north, honking and honking. You want to race them. He makes urgent noises beside you. But the geese, the geese, they are glorious. You hear the crunch before you feel the impact. You lurch forward and the horn goes off when your head hits it. The geese continue on. He gets out to negotiate with the driver. The two men flap their arms wildly.

3. Parenting: Record the milestones. You count to ten, but the kids don't listen. The sink is overflowing with suds, the table still needs clearing, but he's already on his laptop. He has clients now, he says, and they expect him to be working all the time. The house smells like lemon lime and its toxic derivative. The kids start going at each other, furniture their best ammunition. One cushion, then another. *Thump. Thump.* He yells but not at them, at you. Get them to quiet down, he says. I'm *working*. The word is like a weapon. The kids hear it too. You're not like Léa's mom who's always early. Not like Vanessa's mom who bakes cookies. Not like Felix's dad who goes on every field trip and writes the goddamn newsletter. What kind of asshole does that, you think. Now the boys are crying, both of them. You hesitate: you want to scoop them up, pour their livewire bodies into pyjamas, kiss them. But everything you might have had went into the sink, down the drain. *Tabarnac*, he swears, as you herd them to their rooms. No story tonight.

4. Shopping: Make a list before you leave the house. He says it will be a quick stop but you know better. He likes the oversize carts that can be steered with the touch of a well-placed finger. Up and down the aisles you follow. He tosses in clothes, frozen meats, cereal boxes, garden equipment, a toaster. Extra-large slots, big enough for four bagels. He spends money like a magician; this is not the magic you married him for. You find a swinging garden chair, the kind with a canvas overhang, and shut your eyes. The massive klieg lights are thirty feet up and they buzz like hovering locusts. He likes to say *success is just around the corner* at every aisle. You always hope it means no more shopping. But it means *more* shopping. You feel sick. An hour later he retraces his steps calling your name, but what you hear is his embarrassment and anger. You keep one foot on the ground, easing the swing back and forth, back and forth. Row by row the lights shut down with loud *thwanks*. By the time you get out, the parking lot is empty and the wind sighs through your hair like fingers. Empty of cars, of shoppers, of time, the parking lot is beautiful. You don't want to leave, ever.

5. Healthy living: Cook simple meals. He's late again, and that's just how it's going to be. You don't dare text or work yourself up about it. He's got ambitions, goals, new clients, he's doing it for you, can't you understand that? Evidently not. You eat your dinner after the kids go to bed. Then you eat his. This might teach him something about hunger, you think. Then you throw up.

6. Cellphone etiquette: Do not talk about personal details in public. You were lucky to get on the bus. Standing tucked in behind the driver you can't help but lean over two older women. Passengers jostle your backpack so you bring it round front, almost in the women's faces. You mumble apologies. They trade looks. Your phone starts trembling and you scrounge through every pocket and of course it's in the last one. At this moment the bus screeches to a stop and the bag crunches into the four breasts of the two women. You understand the sound of swearing, even in Portuguese. As for him, he's mad. You can tell from the first word, the way he slows his speech, e-nun-ci-a-ting ev-ery syll-a-ble like when you first met and neither of you could speak the other's language. You hold the phone away from your ear because now he is screaming. The Portuguese ladies stop talking. How the hell is he supposed to pick up the kids when he *told* you he had a late meeting and he has to stay at work and it's halfway across town and how do you expect him to get anything done if he has to get to the school by five o'clock and why can't you do it you're not doing anything you're just, what, writing, right? You can't call that a job, he says. You could tell him you're already on your way, but you don't. You could also tell him that you know he doesn't have a meeting. The driver slams the brakes again and your backpack rushes ahead and lands squarely in the first woman's face. She's not worried though, and pats her lap telling you to rest it there. They smile gently, the two old ladies, their eyes twinkling with some kind of understanding.

7. Stand-up comedy: Use your life as inspiration. He doesn't look up from his laptop. It's good you're thinking of getting a job now that the kids are both in school, he says. If you tell him what you are looking for he can help, that's his specialty, and you don't even have to pay him. *Yet*, he grins. You remember when that smile was actually a smile. But you tell him you've already found a job—in Ottawa. You tell him you're going without him, just you and the kids. He doesn't hear that last part, but Ottawa? Ha! he scoffs, Québec should have separated when it had the chance. What do you think you're doing, he asks, separating? Yes, I am separating, you say, I am separating. Then you laugh and laugh and laugh. It's the funniest thing you've said in a long, long time.

THE BEEKEEPER

"**H**oney!"

He hit the brakes hard, throwing them both against their seatbelts. "What?"

"Jesus, Thomas. *Miel,*" she said, pointing behind them. "*Miel* means honey. You didn't see it?"

"Where?" he asked again, looking out the window. "I can't see it."

"You passed it."

That was all she was going to say, Jules decided. The road goes in two directions and the honey is now behind them. It was his idea to look for signs of honey or eggs or anything else they could buy "directly from the source." She caught sight of his concentrated face and thin lips as he turned the car around; she looked the other way so she could roll her eyes. He's worrying about being sideswiped, worried that a vehicle will come out of the turn and split them in half. If he's going to tell that story about how his aunt was killed by a tractor going twenty kilometres an hour that she never saw coming for the millionth time, Jules swore she would kill him herself. But he said nothing, just mouthed *miel* over and over. He puts such effort into being easygoing, she thought.

"Hull-o," Thomas said in a singsong voice and turned into a long driveway. A handmade sign with a painted honey bee hung over the porch: *Miel Mario*. He hesitated before getting out of the car. "Do you think they're home?"

"The sign is out, of course they're home. That's how people around here make their money. Come on."

The crunch of the gravel got a dog going. They could hear it barking and jumping against the front door like it wanted to tear a leg off, and could, and had. A deep voice yelled at it to shut up. The living room window's blinds crinkled. Jules and Thomas stood on either side of the car, hesitant, perhaps fearful. "Maybe we should go," Thomas offered.

A man opened the front door and stood outside in the shade of the porch. *"Je peux vous aider?"*

"Bonjour!" Thomas put his hand up to shield his eyes from the sun bouncing off the tin roof. *"Miel?"*

Jules was sure she could see the man roll his eyes as he switched languages. "For sure," he said. His face, hard and rigid, softened on command, the lines around his eyes relaxing as if he was born smiling. Jules watched the transformation; she knew about men using their faces like fugitives use lanterns in a cave. "Follow me, it's just over here," he said, stepping out and leading them around back.

Behind the house, fifteen columns of white wooden crates sat neatly in rows, each high as a person, a grid of order against the wild field and forest around them. Tight swarms of bees hovered above the boxes like army drones. Jules stopped in her tracks.

"Oh my god," she said, whispering. "I'm not walking through the bees." The beekeeper looked back, cocked his head as if impatient. Then he lifted his hands and smiled. It's nothing, he seemed to say.

"Come on, Jules," Thomas took his wife's elbow. "Look, he says it's fine."

They moved forward under the man's gaze. It occurred to Jules that the beekeeper was enjoying their trepidation, their city stupidity. It must be the entertainment around here. Beside her, Thomas shuffled awkwardly on his heels. She knew he was protecting his shoes; they hadn't thought ahead and now he was tromping through dirt in his expensive Italian Velascas. The beekeeper, on the other hand, was shod in heavy leather boots whose seams strained at the steel toe plates, their weight giving him an animalistic gait. In spite of the uneven ground, he was lithe and sure, the *thrump thrump* of his feet in the rough dirt sounding like it was borne of nature. In contrast, Jules thought her husband walked like a cartoon mouse.

They arrived at a shed attached to the back of the house. Thomas hurried to catch up to the beekeeper and disappeared inside after him. Jules reached out to grab the door, but Thomas let go and it slammed shut in front of her face. She stood still as speckled chickens guarded the ground around her like tin soldiers. *Goddammit Thomas*, she said out loud, their bickering long past needing privacy. It had been his idea to take the slow roads back to Ottawa from Montreal. Let's see some countryside, he said. He went on about farming and markets and pricing and commodities, which was rich for a man whose hands didn't see anything more challenging than an uncooperative spreadsheet. A hen approached, and before it could make contact, she stomped her foot and ducked inside.

Hot as it was outside, it was twice that in the honey shed. Four stainless steel vats lined the wall, each with a spigot and a bucket. Off to the side, a dozen bee boxes were pulled apart on two long tables, laying this way and that, thick pools of honey congealing on the counter and on the floor. Bits of discarded honeycomb were piled on another table, while other pieces lay about on a framed screen and drained into a smaller vat. Dead bees and flies stuck to it all, in pieces and whole. Others, alive and frantic, flew at the windows like tiny missiles. Between them and the noisy fan in the corner, the din was intense. Thomas peered into a vat, touched the honeycombs, licked his fingers.

"You come on a good day," the beekeeper said. "I have spring stock left. It is very clear, see?" He held up a jar and yes, it was almost perfectly clear.

"Look at that, honey," Thomas giggled. "I meant you, honey, not the jar of honey. Get it?"

Not bothering to hide a smirk, the beekeeper looked at Jules as if to make common cause.

"I called her honey," Thomas explained. "That must be a workplace hazard around here!"

Jules cringed. As Thomas peered into the next vat, his voice echoing in the metal chamber, the beekeeper never broke eye contact with her. While she generally had no difficulty hanging her husband out to dry for a good laugh, making alliance with the beekeeper felt suddenly dangerous. She hoped that maybe this was just a fun dangerous, the fun for a laugh kind. The beekeeper aimed a tiny spoon at her mouth. "My spring honey."

The hand that held the spoon looked like it had been hurriedly bandaged, a strip of cotton wound roughly around and tied at the palm. A blood stain had seeped through at the knuckles. Jules took a tiny step back.

"Thank you, I can do this." She was careful not to touch his fingers.

The beekeeper sucked in his breath while she brought the spoon to her mouth, so she looked away at Thomas bent over the third vat. Something was not feeling right, not feeling right at all. If Thomas also hesitated maybe she could believe herself, maybe she could put the spoon down and they could just turn around and leave. Sorry, no cash! they'd say. Or something about diabetes. They never even ate honey. Honey had no value in their house, it was a plastic bear that crystallized in the back of the cupboard. But Thomas raised his eyebrows, smiled brighter, urged her to taste. His shine was familiar, it was important to him that the beekeeper not be left waiting. For one long second, her disappointment in her husband flared dangerously close to hatred. She put the spoon in her mouth.

"Mostly apple flowers," the beekeeper said. "And some clover. Can you taste it?"

Thomas took the next spoon and sucked noisily.

"Hey yeah! I can taste the apples. Can you, honey?"

The lines on the beekeeper's face ran in perfect verticals, as if their purpose was to quickly siphon him of emotion, like an expertly drained field.

"Yes," she said.

Thomas picked up an empty two-litre tub and gestured to the beekeeper. "Do you mind if I fill this myself?" The man grinned at Jules and shrugged. Thomas turned away and opened a spigot. "Honey!" He was entranced.

"Best honey in the region." The beekeeper leaned against the door jamb. Jules would have not thought his thick frame could be so lanky, elegant even in its menace. He ran a jar under her nose. "Smell."

As she leaned towards the jar, Jules saw something move in the house behind him. Half hidden by a gauzy curtain appliquéd with cutouts of fruit, a woman was watching them. Jules stared back and, even though the woman's eyes were vaguely blurred shadows, she recognized something in the gaze that chilled her. Then she made an almost imperceptible gesture with her hands, a sign of some sort. Jules leaned forward for a better look.

The beekeeper followed Jules's eyes—and exhaled a low growl. Distracted, Thomas looked up from his bucket, letting honey seep out over his shoes.

"Oh my god oh crap." Thomas lifted first one foot then the other. "I'm so sorry. Uh, Jules, my shoes!"

"*Merde.*" The beekeeper grabbed a rag. "Câlisse de merde."

Jules looked back into the kitchen but the woman had backed up and was now a blur. The beekeeper, cleaning the floor, kept his eyes on the window, his jaw working like a grindstone. Her stomach sank with a brick of fear.

"*Qu'est-cé qu't'as vu, toi?*"

"What? I didn't see anything."

"*Mêle-toi de tes affaires!*" He threw the rag down and barged into the house.

"What did he say?" Thomas asked. "I hope he's not making a big deal about it. I mean, it's only honey, I'll pay him for it. On the other hand, my shoes are worth..."

"*Quiet, Thomas.*"

Behind the apple and lemon cutouts, Jules watched the man grab the woman's arm, his voice now a train yard of scrapes and rasps. The woman said something in a plaintive tone, but he growled her down. The dog barked, but it was growled down too. The beekeeper dragged the woman by the arm and left the room. She took one last look at Jules before disappearing and raised her hand as if in greeting—or for help.

"I don't like this," said Jules. "I want to go."

Thomas was dabbing at his shoes. "Don't worry about it. I'll live."

"Thomas, we have to go."

From inside the house the unmistakable sound of a slap rang out.

"Now."

"Almost done here."

Suddenly, a loud *crack* burst through the air, followed by another, followed by silence and the ringing of their ears. The dog whimpered, but then he was quiet too.

"Oh my god."

Thomas looked up. "What was that?"

"Thomas, let's get the fuck out of here." Jules ran to the door, her legs tingling with fear. Thomas had only a vague but growing understanding that his wife was afraid, that the beekeeper had been menacing, that something was happening. "Oh shit," he finally said.

"Exactly. Let's go."

Thomas dropped the bucket and followed his wife. Jules ran ahead, rounded the house and was halfway down the driveway to the car when Thomas stopped running. He slowed his pace along the side of the house, his head in line with the three windows, one after another. Jules, about to run back to grab him, halted when she could see someone keeping pace with him from inside the house. *Honey*, he barely whispered at the second window. By the third, he was a sitting duck. Jules could see that the person was carrying something. A shotgun? Yes, that's exactly what that sound had been. Jules knew. Jules already perfectly sure of the massive danger that now covered them like a swarm of furious bees. The beekeeper was carrying a gun. Thomas felt a fear he never knew existed. Movies only aroused an approximate version of it—fear embodied in a look, a scream. But this was something else entirely. This overtook his entire being, from the edges of his skin to the knots of his bowels to a searing emptying of his brain. This was a complete invasion of panic. He ran.

Jules was at the car first. Thomas, a few seconds behind, opened the door and jumped in. "Get in the car! Let's go! Let's go!"

But she suddenly had gone from all motion to complete stillness. She remained outside the car and stared back at the house. She whispered to her husband. "*Wait*."

He opened the passenger door and tried to pull her in. *Get in get in get in get in*. He kept pushing the start button but the engine resisted. "Jesus Christ, Jules, let's go!" He wouldn't look up. She pulled her arm out of his grip and headed towards the house.

"Jules!" He screamed.

Someone was standing on the porch, something in their hands, holding something aloft. It wasn't a gun and it wasn't the beekeeper. It was his wife.

Jules took the bucket of honey from the woman. She pulled out her wallet and counted some cash. She went back in her purse and gave the woman something else, her business card: *Julia Malek, Criminal Defense Law.* They huddled together and spoke. All that could be heard from the car was the softness of their voices and the remote buzzing of bees against windows. Then they hugged.

It wasn't until they were back on the highway that Thomas was able to speak. "What did she say to you?"

"Nothing."

"What do you mean nothing? What did she say? What happened? What was that bang? Where did the honey man go? And the dog, for god's sake, the dog. Jules? What happened?" His emotions were weighted with tears and anguish, so he kept them at bay with more questions. "Was someone hurt? Jules, you know what I'm talking about." He banged at the steering wheel. "Dammit!"

But Jules stared out the window.

"Jules!"

"Nothing, Thomas. Nothing happened. She wanted to make sure we didn't leave without our honey. That's what we came for, after all."

They were going to learn to love honey, she decided.

MOTIONLESS

It was just me and a lime-less bottle of Corona on the front stoop as a steady stream of panting dogs and texting owners headed towards Mont Royal. The sky was darkening when your urgent voice approached from behind. I finished off the beer while you caught your breath.

"There's a barn owl out back!"

Truth may take its time, but you never lie or exaggerate so I followed you inside. On the balcony next door, Sylvie was hopping from one foot to the other, pointing.

It was smaller than I'd pictured an owl to be, ten inches high at best, its feathers a mess of beiges and browns. For some reason I thought it looked like a bureaucrat. "Where's its briefcase?" I laughed.

"It was lying down at first," Sylvie said, looking at you.

"But then it stood up," you said, staring back at her.

"And it's been standing up ever since," you both said.

It rankled me, this shared excitement. Sylvie's voice a little too high, your concern for the owl a little too intense.

"How do you know it's a barn owl?" You dismissed the question, making that *bof* noise you picked up from watching *Tout le monde en parle* with Sylvie. You went into the house and returned with oven mitts.

Sylvie was all *ben oui!* as she disappeared into her kitchen and emerged with a cat cage. You both ran down and she passed it over the fence, tossing it the final distance. You caught it with a finesse that pained me to watch.

"Now what?" I had to ask. "Once the owl is in the cage what are you going to do then?"

"Call around," Sylvie said. "Maybe the SPCA will take it."

"Yes," you said, cooing at the bird, moving slowly toward it with your outstretched orange oven mitts, Sylvie now on our side of the fence, crouching behind you. "Can you call somebody?" you asked me. Then you returned your gaze to Sylvie, "Or you? Maybe it's easier if you call?"

"It's fine," I said. "I can speak French just fine." I went inside and called the SPCA who told me to call Le Berger Blanc who told me to call a vet. I googled numbers and found someone who treated exotic animals. She in turn told me to call a woman who took in wild birds. I called her. She said to bring the bird in right away.

"Where are you located?" I asked.

"Saint-Hyacinthe."

"That's like sixty kilometres away!"

"If you don't bring the bird in now it will die. Do you have a cage?"

"Yes, in fact we just—"

"Do you have a car?"

"Yes, but—"

"Bring the owl in right away. I will wait for you."

You and Sylvie were talking softly to the feathered civil servant. Neither of you looked up when I delivered the news that I had found a bird lady in godforsaken Saint-Hyacinthe.

"Great," you said.

"Great? It's getting dark and it'll take an hour to get there." I held up a scrap piece of paper. "Her directions were super vague. Turn here, turn there. We'll never find it. She sounded strange. I think she's German."

"I think it's scared," Sylvie said to you. "It must be in pain."

I looked inside. "He looks fine to me. Nice and quiet. Just what you want in an owl. Maybe he's waiting for the meeting to start."

"You need to take the owl to the bird lady," Sylvie said, still looking at you but talking to me, her kindergarten teacher eyes all round and wet.

"Me? Why don't you go? After all, the two of you found the thing together, it's your baby."

"I'd love to," Sylvie said, oblivious to my sarcasm. "But I have to put Lucas to bed. And Jean-François is out." She looked at you and you looked away.

"Maybe it's dead," I suggested, trying another tactic. "How do you know it's not dead? Don't birds die when you touch them? Don't they kill each other when one of them's been touched by a human? Maybe you're giving it a death sentence."

"It's not dead, it just has a broken wing."

"How do you know it has a broken wing?"

"It's obvious," you said in a half whisper. "Or it would have flown away."

You leaned over the owl with a tenderness usually meant for lovers and, oven mitts for pillows, you gently put it in the cage. You carried the cage to the car and strapped it in the back seat. Then you sat beside it.

"It's not a baby," I said. "You can sit in the front." You didn't budge.

It took us an hour and a half to get there—the extra half hour because of all the wrong turns I made because I don't trust GPS. I have trust fatigue. I turned on the radio but you said the talking was disturbing the owl. I played some music but you said it was disturbing the owl. I opened the window because it was hot and it was too early in the season for AC. But it was disturbing the owl.

Saint-Hyacinthe used to be a farming village at the foot of a mountain, but now it was another satellite suburb of Montreal. Bird lady lived in one of the older developments where every house pretended it was alone on the edge of the forest. We rang the doorbell several times. Impatient, we went around back to find a menagerie of cages, sheds, crates of this and that, piles here and there of scattered boards. A chorus of cicadas and bullfrogs strummed from the dark woods. Footsteps sounded from inside the house.

"You have owl? Bring in here."

Startled, we followed a stout grey-haired woman through a labyrinth of sheds lit by bald light bulbs and littered with straw. At least two dozen cages of small animals and birds lined the walls. I wanted to make a joke about Dr Moreau and genetic experiments but held my tongue. That kind of joke works best with a German accent, and no one would have laughed, least of all you.

She took the cage out of your hands and knocked it about here and there as she looked for a clear spot on the counter. You jumped at every bang. She pulled the bird out and set it down, her fingers deftly probing its skin, feathers, claws, beak, tail. "What was it doing when you found it?"

"Nothing," you said. "Just sitting there."

"They are motionless birds."

That sounded like a strange way to describe an animal that, after all, flies. "A motionless bird?" I tried hard to think of a joke but came up with nothing. "What do you mean?"

"Saw-whet owls can be motionless for long periods and appear tame." The German lady's eyes were a dark disconcerting blue. "Do not get fooled." Her hands, burrowed under the owl's wings, stopped moving. "It has a broken wing. Come back in two days and pick it up."

"Okay," you said obediently.

"Pick it up? Why?"

"I will bandage it. It needs to rest and calm down," Bird Fraulein said. "You come back in two days to get your owl."

"Okay," you said.

"But it's not *our owl*," I protested. "What the heck are we going to do with a barn owl?"

"Saw-whet owl," she corrected me. A generation earlier she would have rapped my knuckles with a strap. She put it back in its cage. "They are small and sometimes get lost. Leave me this cage, I am running out. Where do you live?"

"In Montreal, near the mountain," I said.

You stared at her, eyes wide as if responsible for the bird's transgression. "Maybe he lives on the mountain?"

"Maybe," she nodded. She wrote something down and handed it to me. A bill: $375 for fixing the owl, plus the two days' stay. I looked at you but you were sticking your fingers in the cage, making pigeon noises. "Pay me in two days," the bird lady said.

"But what if we don't want it? Can we just leave it here? Can't you set it free? Here?" I gestured to the

Hansel and Gretel forest behind her house. There was no way I wanted to drive back out to Saint-Hyacinthe again. "I don't give a hoot about the owl," I said, laughing at myself. But you whacked my arm. "Fine," I mumbled.

"He lives on the mountain. He will know where to go if you take him," the bird lady said.

The drive home seemed quick, which was a relief. It was late, I knew my way, maybe you dozed. All I know is by the time I found a parking spot on our street, I had it all figured out.

The next day I waited for you to come home from work, to put your things down, to go to the bathroom, fill up the kettle, gaze over the balcony into Sylvie's apartment, call out to her. When you came out of the kitchen, I was ready.

"The bird lady phoned today," I said.

"Oh?" You perked up, anxious, expectant, hopeful.

"The owl died during the night. There was nothing she could do."

"No!" You sat down and put your head in your hands. "The poor thing. The poor, poor thing."

"Yes. Breaks cause trauma to the heart, especially for birds whose hearts are tiny. Their hearts explode. That's what happened." Your face melted with every word. "She said that if you had found her sooner you could have saved her."

I let you cry, but I was resentful of those tears. "Or maybe you shouldn't have touched her at all."

It was like I cracked open a door to a brilliant light, suddenly the only light in the room. "Just because owls are motionless it doesn't mean they need you to help them. You saw it from the balcony but you should have ignored it. It was having its own busy day and doing nothing was part of it. Right? But you had to have it, you had to touch it."

"Oh my god," you whispered.

"It has a family and now the baby owls will be wondering where it is. You need to leave our wild neighbours alone."

But you are not a code breaker, my words were not landing.

"Oh my god," you continued. "I killed it. It's true. I shouldn't have even touched it."

"Sometimes curiosity ruins everything."

You sat on the couch for a long time. You said something every now and then, but I had gone out to the front stoop with a bottle of beer. I should have been making dinner, it was my turn, but I couldn't get up.

Then you went next door.

THE PLOW

Marc woke up with one arm under her, the other over, and a leg across her shins. Like bears stirring in a cave, the tiny hairs on her skin intermingled with his own, conserving heat. He dressed in the dark, sprayed the toilet bowl—for which she always forgave him—brushed his teeth. In the kitchen, the layers of sweaters, jackets and pants stiffened his limbs, slowed him down, then heated him up. He ate fast, left quickly. The cold didn't hit him until he turned the key. The old Honda was a freezer on wheels, and it took the entire trip to the terminal, almost twenty kilometres, for the engine to heat up. By the time he climbed into the cabin of the snowplow his back and kidneys were aching. It was minus 29 Celsius not counting wind chill.

He drove quickly with the blade up. The seat bounced hard with every rut. The night was black and yellow, the streets empty save for a taxi or two. A gang of teenage boys walked in the middle of the road as if on parade. He knew the uniform: bomber jackets, baseball caps, running shoes. Their hands were plunged deep in their frozen denim pockets, shoulders wrapped around necks like scarves. Winter had transformed them into figures of cold energy and menace, casting moon shadows in ways only boys can. He turned onto a smaller street. He didn't know the neighbourhood but after a couple of snowstorms it would be as familiar as his own. Small and narrow streets of single family homes built after the Second World War. That's what Serge had told him, and Serge only knew because his wife had grown up there. He had been expecting something a little more upscale—Serge was obviously easily impressed—but as he lowered the blade he was relieved to see old cars, single-pane windows, unrepaired fences, rotting balconies. He'd tell Marie-Claire. Neither of them had family in Montreal, so they could set their sights anywhere. Just a simple place to raise a kid, maybe two, hopefully three. Somewhere to settle back into her skin, their shared fur skin, her legs vined around his arms rooting together in the cave of their collective breathing.

The blade jumped up too fast and crashed down too hard. The entire cabin rattled, a steel against steel quaking he didn't like one bit. Something flew by on his right into the snow behind him. An animal maybe—a raccoon, he suspected. Serge said there were lots of raccoons out here because of the fields and empty lots. But the colour was off, it seemed brighter in the streetlamp, maybe even red. Blood? Or a coat? A red coat. He screeched to a halt and looked around. Snow was careening hard off the bank and had already covered the newly cleared road with a thin drift. It swirled in through the top of the jammed window and wrapped around his torso. He pulled his arms close and wondered about getting out for a quick tour around the machine. But with the wheel up against the bank, he'd have to climb over it, slip step by step, balance on the frame of the blade as the engine squalled. He'd never admit it, but he hated being close to its roaring engine. In any case, he'd done plenty of walkarounds before and for what. For nothing. After a minute, he nudged the plow forward. He picked up speed at the corner and finished the route in no time. She was eating breakfast when he got home. There was an egg for him and some toast, a pot of coffee. She kissed him softly on her way out and reminded him to pay the phone bill. He took his plate to the living room and looked out the front window. He wondered about his chances of getting a route closer to home. He wondered who would wear a red coat. Only a woman would wear a red coat. He impatiently scraped the rest of his breakfast into the garbage.

Seventy thousand tons of salt, eight hundred trucks, thousands of hours in overtime, Montreal's budget blown and winter had barely begun. How long would it last this year? Could be a melt in February followed by only a few stubborn heaves in March. Or could be a pileup until April, so much snow that the rivers rise up and break into building-sized sea blocks, crackling day and night as the muddy glaciers break off and move upshore. He'd seen it out by Valleyfield, out by Rigaud, out by Chambly, modest rivers violated by nature's icebreaker. He'd made piles of money then. That's how they had the down payment for a house and that's how she'd finally said yes. He was doing everything right. See? Proof, he said to his old friends, anyone can change, even me. They laughed and took bets. He napped in the afternoon so he could be up when she came home. She made them an early dinner, a heavy greasy meaty dinner just for him. He dozed in front of the television while she cleaned up. Later, her hands roamed his body like a light breeze and he fought his fatigue, wanting to respond, wanting to be like bending grasses against her gentle plowing. But he fell into an even deeper sleep and she loved him for it. She was not used to men like this. He woke up a few hours later to her soft snores. He stowed his desire like a treasure, saving it for later, untangled his limbs, got out of bed.

The guys were hovering over the coffee pot. Serge was reading the *Journal* aloud, punctuating the text with commentary. Five foot three, thirty-eight years old—*ben* she looks fifty in this photo!—two kids, works at the Bar Chantalle in Lasalle. He wondered what this was all about. She's missing, said Serge. He turned the paper around so everyone could see her picture. So? he asked. So, she was coming home from the bar and no one saw her again. She's missing.

He didn't like the way everyone was quiet, the way they looked at him. You didn't see anything, Serge asked. You didn't hear anything? Did you know she lives on your route? Did you notice people leaving Bar Chantalle when you drove by? What the hell. *No*, I didn't see anything! He poured the rest of his coffee down the sink and stomped towards his truck. She was wearing a red coat, Serge called out. Did you see anyone with a red coat? Serge was an asshole, always an asshole. But he was also a tease and Marc was too far to hear everyone laughing. They loved to rile each other up, jab at that place that was softest, most vulnerable, most afraid. They'd hunt it down, yank it into the light and watch it shrink in horror. They were the men who drove monsters through the darkened streets while the rest of the world slept, trusting their thick hands to turn the right way, change the gear at the right time, lift the blade just so. They told no one, but they were afraid, always afraid. Leading behemoth machines that never forgave, that made them pay for their sins. He started the truck and then stopped it again, got back out and ran to the bathroom to empty his insides. Later, the seat bounced even harder, landing with bone-shattering smashes each and every time, as if the voided weight had made all the difference between comfort and torment.

He said nothing to her over breakfast. She wanted to see the *Journal*, which he usually brought home, but he told her he had forgotten it. She wasn't happy about missing the paper because apparently a nine-year-old girl was all set to win *La Voix*, not to mention the fact that the girl's parents were in the middle of a messy divorce due to one of them getting a sex change. He didn't see the connection but she laughed. Of course there's a connection. He shook his head. How long is winter going to last this year. How long is winter going to last this year. How long is winter going to last this year. She stared at him.

The snow pounded and pounded and pounded. Heavy flakes came straight at him like parachuting soldiers, the wipers charging angrily ahead. He rumbled along the autoroute, an impatient trail of white lights behind him. He laughed at the idiots who maneuvered to get in front and then fishtailed on the unsalted road. *Osti de gang de caves*, he said out loud. He was comfortable now. The cab was warm and he just had to drive. He marveled at the snowflakes. Each one tiny and insignificant but together they converged into a massive and brutal army.

The woman was still in the paper. In spite of the absence of news or clues, the *Journal* decided to take on the cause. They narrowed down and itemized her last moments and interviewed every possible person with a connection. She had worked late at the bar, closed it up, parted with a colleague. He had offered a drive home but she was okay, she told him, she only lived three blocks away. The last he saw her was in his rear-view mirror, he was quoted, standing in the bar parking lot as if waiting to take the first step. She had been wearing a long, red parka with a fake fur-lined hood, might have been listening to music, he couldn't quite remember if she had ear buds or not. There were two teenagers at home, the father lived in Verdun and worked as a mechanic. He was married again, had two more kids, younger ones, babies. Any possibility of his involvement was duly raised then dismissed. He threatened to sue the *Journal*. It was his week with the kids and he had gone straight home. They left the *Journal* on the table when they went for their shift, forgot all about it. Marc picked up every single copy and threw them in the garbage.

He crouched down and looked under his truck, ran his hands along the wheel well, felt under the chassis as far as he could go, looked for fabric, thread, bits of cloth. Ran his fingers over and along every inch. Wondered if he had been born blind would his fingertips be more sensitive, feel what was not there, feel her breath, hear her cry as she flew into a wall of steel and smoke.

What are you doing? Serge stood behind him. Serge would sell you to the devil or the dépanneur if it suited him. Did you get into an accident or something, did you forget to fill out an accident report, is there something I should know? Nothing, Marc said, straightening up. He knew how to deal with assholes. He knew it in his bones, was raised on it. When you never have family you don't need enemies, someone had once said. Serge laughed and walked away. Marc's insides shook and for the second time that week he emptied his breakfast, lunch and supper into the garage toilet.

It was too hot in the bed but she kept putting her arms and legs on him. He moved them off but she stirred and put them back. He looked at his phone: he didn't have to get up for another hour. She moved her face to his shoulder, both legs on his. He swore and got up. What did she want from him anyways, he wondered for the first time. Someone safe? reliable? a good man? How did she know he was a good man? He yanked up his pants and regretted where his mind was taking him. She'd had a tough ride. She said he was the first man to love her and not want to rip her apart in the process. He couldn't begrudge her that. You have a good heart, she whispered once. He'd been so surprised to hear it, like it was another language. You make me want to be good, he answered after a long minute of hiding his eyes. Now he felt a melting and, for a strange and discomfiting second, thought he was going to cry. He swore out loud, louder, louder. He left the house and, forgetting everything, banged the door behind him.

He took a detour, stopped the truck. Walked over to the snowbank and kicked it. Realized that people might see him, that in spite of it being 3:10 in the morning, there might be someone wondering why the snowplow driver was kicking the snowbank right where the woman from Bar Chantalle went missing. So he dropped his glove and then made as if to find it and pick it up. He waved it around theatrically, put it back on his hand. Felt like an idiot. He hated whoever could be in their window, a hate he could almost taste, a coppery tang that shocked him with its familiarity. *Crisse*, he didn't want to go there. That was then and this is now goddammit. Got a good job found a good woman deserved a good life. He kicked the snowbank and exhaled into a growl. No one heard.

He tried to remember. The blade bouncing off the packed snow with a jarring bang, something flying off to the side then gone. Fluttering like fabric, not like a raccoon, heavy fabric, a coat, red. He had twisted around to look but whatever it was was gone. The remembering competed with the music so he turned it off. It was hot in the cab now, he pulled off his ear protectors and then his scarf. With his ears exposed, the noise shocked him with its heft, the sound of working gears and pistons and pneumatic thrusting. So much metal, so much weight.

His bones and insides rattled as the chair bounced up and down. That had been the fun part when he first started. Now *this* was a job. This was something he could do, rumble down the roads in the black of night and push that wall of snow with all his weight. It made him feel strong and purposeful for the first time in his life. Like a coat whose job it is to keep a woman warm, thick fabric, not a raccoon, most certainly red.

He refused breakfast, third morning in a row. But you have to eat, she insisted. A red scarf was wrapped around her neck as she readied for work. Didn't he know that breakfast was the most important meal of the day? *Tabarnac!* Are you stupid? This is my *supper.* I have to go to sleep while the rest of the world has a life to live. He pushed the plate away so roughly it landed on the floor. She opened her eyes wide. A dormant part of him took pleasure as an inchoate beast sparked to frightening life. She shut the bedroom door behind her, one hand trembling ever so slightly.

Someone had put up pictures of Angèle. What the fuck kind of name was that, he wondered. Every lamppost and mailbox had a picture of her, and if he drove by quickly enough it played out like a movie. Angèle, Angèle, Angèle. He pushed down on the accelerator and ran over a mailbox. Two streets away he got out and inspected the truck for dents or bits of paint. Nothing, so fuck you, Serge.

The most recent *Journal* article was taped up in the kitchen. The guys worried about her now. Someone had a brother who knew her sister. They could afford to be solemn, he thought, easy for them. They're all losers. He tore it down. Hey, what are you doing, Serge asked. What do you care about her for, he demanded. Eh? Who cares about some Bar Chantalle slut. And Angèle, what the fuck kind of name is that? It's a stripper name. They looked at him, saw something they had seen in each other, in the mirror even, but never in him. They had thought he was one of the good guys and it made them proud, made them proud of possibilities for themselves. We're all just good guys, they could say, just simple guys who want a simple life. Now his face was screwed up and his voice was loud and the veins in his neck throbbed with visible anger. They backed away. They got in their cabs and covered their ears.

He found out where she lived and drove by her house. He stopped the truck. So what? City trucks do nothing all the time. That made him smile. He's just another lazy city worker, and who the fuck cares. He sipped his coffee. She was thirty-eight and had been wearing a red coat. Eight years older than him, he only had black coats no kids one cat, not black not red but orange. She never made it home but was lying in the snowbank a block away. Then he froze with panic. Winter was not going to last forever. One day the snow will melt and she will be discovered. Frozen and mangled in such a way that the only conclusion will be that a snowplow was the culprit. He knew how things like that went down. A minute scrap of yellow paint on her boot, on her hand, maybe nudged between two teeth, and they'd find him. He'd be charged with negligence, hit and run, manslaughter, murder. His entire life would be ruined, he'd be back in hell with no way out and no one to love him. Marie-Claire would look at him not only with disgust but, worse, disappointment. He jammed down on the accelerator and the beast careened around the corner and down the road, onto another road, another corner, missed a parked car by inches, and stopped with a thud at the snowbank. Here.

He backed up, faced into it, rammed his blade. Backed up, angled a little to the left, rammed his blade. Backed up, angled more, rammed. Backed up, angled, rammed. He kept at it until he carved out an area the length of half a dozen cars, pushed the snow so resolutely that grass could be seen underneath. First grass in months. The next morning kids on their way to school would jump up and down on it, touch its frozen lace. So resolutely was the snow pushed back that it covered a walkway and hid a front door. He wondered who lived there. Depending on their attitude, they could make a stink. Later that morning he went straight to the bedroom. She was doing something with her clothes or jewelry, he couldn't tell what. Happy to see him she went for a kiss, hot arms around his neck. He pushed her away and crawled under the blankets. Well at least take off your clothes, she said, I just changed the sheets. Fuck the sheets, he mumbled, and fell asleep. He dreamt he told her everything but then she put on a red coat, grew another head, devoured him.

Serge waved him to a stop, motioned him down from the cab. What the hell you doing plowing a wall in front of a house? It was such a strange thing to do that right now Serge was more curious than angry. Listen, if there's anything going on, if there's anything I should know. How's Marie-Claire? How're things? No way, Marc thought to himself. No way you get to ask me about her. Everything's fine, he said out loud. She's fine and I'm fine. Have you seen the fucking snow outside? If people can't deal with it they can go to Florida. I plowed the snow so they can drive their fucking cars to their fucking jobs. Now they want it manicured? Serge raised his eyebrows, raised his hands, walked away. Another hothead, he could hear Serge muttering. Another fucking hothead.

Marc returned to the snowbank at the end of his shift. The street was alive with people, dogs, cars, school buses, noise. His head was light and empty, ready for sleep. How strange, he thought. Darkness can give you the impression that the world is yours, but daylight reveals that it belongs to everyone else. He stopped a block away and walked to the wall of snow that was pushed up against the house. He chuckled, it *was* a bit extreme. The door flew open. An old man yelled in Italian-accented French. In spite of the raised voice and shaking fist, he was relieved. Just an old guy in stained pants. He nodded sympathetically and pretended to be taking his complaint. The old man finally went back inside. He kicked around in the snow and felt a wave of dizziness. He thought he saw something red but it turned out to be the plastic end of a sled. He could hardly breathe.

Marie-Claire was waiting for him. Are you seeing someone else, she asked. That woke him up. Are you fucking kidding me? He tried not to swear in front of her. Are you kidding me? When? Where? I come home every day, I sleep with you. She had to acknowledge that, but logistics did not fill the gap that her instinct sensed. There was something going on, she said. He could see her fight her own tears and for a second felt a fierce pride. Fine, she said, but a hardness in her voice had taken hold. If it isn't a woman then what is it? She waited for him to say something, but he didn't. Fine, she said. I don't need this. She left him with breakfast and lunch and the car insurance renewal papers. He ate neither and tore up the bill.

He went back to the snowbank and idled in his truck. The old Italian opened the door and yelled. Didn't he have anything better to do? Go back in the house old man, he shouted. He did it differently this time, kept the blade high and scraped backwards. He dug through the snow like an archeologist at Giza. It had meant absolutely nothing to him when they learned about the pyramids at school. Some place, some history, some lost land of sand. But here he was at an icy monolith, feeling like one of the workers pushing and rolling the snow back and forth. No, he was a Pharaoh, a great leader, showing the people how it's done. The vague memory made him wonder exactly what the pyramids were used for. Something about burying the Pharaohs? The cold was getting to him so he dialed up the heat in the cab.

What the flying fuck, Serge yelled as he got out of the truck. When Serge got mad he spoke half in English, he'd heard him do it before. What the hell do you think you're doing? What is going on? Serge wouldn't let up, he couldn't even get a word in. I got two complaints tonight, two! One from the same guy and one from his neighbour. What the fuck? I got the city breathing down my neck, the councillor breathing down my neck, the fucking union breathing down my neck. And you, you're acting like a weirdo. I'm asking you nicely now Marc, what the fuck is going on. You losing it? Drinking? Marc looked at Serge and unzipped his jacket. Unfurled his scarf. Kicked the snow off his boots. He said nothing. But Serge's eyes got harder. Fine, Serge said. This one's going in your file. One more complaint and you're out. On your fucking ass.

Marie-Claire stood over his sleeping body. Fuck you, she said softly, and left for work. He opened his eyes and shot up, layered himself, two for his feet, two for his legs, three for his torso, then the coat. Not red, but black. Coffee was waiting for him: one, two, a third. He returned to the snowbank. It was daylight, he was in his own car, everything would be different. He retrieved his shovel from the trunk and got to work. Five minutes later the Italian came out in his boots and coat. Not red. Didn't yell. Mark glanced up but otherwise paid no attention. Then the Italian started blathering like he was talking to someone. A crazy, Marc thought. I just call police, the old guy said. Marc stood up and groaned. His back was sore, his hands were cold, snot was running down his face. The snow was hard, like a wall. He remembered crawling in a snow cave once and hiding for the entire day. His breath had made a soft film of ice around the inside walls, strengthening them, keeping in the heat. He should have stayed there his entire childhood. The Italian lurched forward and grabbed Marc's shovel. You go, he said, you get out of here! They tussled back and forth until the old guy fell forward on his face. What do you expect, Marc yelled at him, frustrated that he had been forced to wrestle an old man. He nudged at him with his boot. Come on, get up *tabarnac*. But the body was as inert and heavy as the snowbank. Fuuuuck, he yelled to himself. He thrust the shovel again and again into the snow. Fuuuuck. A police car screeched to a halt. Snow was on his face, down his neck, up his stomach, breaching the layers, cold rivulets on his skin. They pushed him into the back seat. An ambulance arrived a minute later and loaded the Italian onto a stretcher.

Marc had no answers for them at the station. Why was he digging into the snowbank? Why had he made the snowbank in the first place? He resisted calling Marie-Claire. No sense calling a lawyer, he didn't know the first thing about finding a lawyer. Anyways, they hadn't charged him with anything. What, arrest him for plowing too hard? He wasn't even thinking of the red coat. He looked around the station. The officers were like teenagers, their noses stuck in their cellphones. He looked at the printouts of various missing people. Then he saw the poster for Angèle. He glanced around and met someone's eyes, a police officer he hadn't noticed before. So what happened to her, he asked as casually as possible. Did you ever find who killed her? The cop got up and tore it down.

Have you solved the case then? Marc was incredulous. Nah, they found her. Found the body? The cop looked at him now, something strange about this guy. No, he told Marc, they found her, she had just run off with some guy for a few days. What? Yeah, she turned up with some guy she met on the Internet. Why do you want to know? Nothing, Marc said, we all followed her story in the *Journal*. Yeah, this shit happens all the time, the cop said. She went to Arizona or something like that, go figure, and she has kids. Marc had to sit down to catch his breath. Another cop came in from outside and they whispered. The first turned to him. Mr Del Fiacco is dead, he said. Who? The guy you beat up, he's dead. They cuffed him.

When Marc didn't call or come home, she didn't panic. She knew then and there that the trust was broken, all bridges down. She packed up her things, took that overtime due her, and went to Trois-Rivières. She'd set up at her mother's apartment for a bit, figure things out, get back on her feet. She cried for three days, maybe four. Her mother never liked him, didn't she say? Never liked the look of him. Darkness doesn't go away just because you turn on a light, she'd said. They were eating dinner in front of the television when they saw him on the screen, a mug shot, followed by a picture of Vincenzo Del Fiacco, age eighty-one. The union was blaming it on the intensity of back to back blizzards and the stress of overtime, and that Del Fiacco's stroke could have happened at any time. So, not a woman at all. Not anything but despair. Her mother recoiled. Did she have anything to do with this? Is she in hiding? Marie-Claire did not have the energy to deal with her mother's negative view of the world and everything in it. She packed her bag again.

Marie-Claire paid his bail, took him home, ran a bath, put on the kettle, didn't ask a single question, answers would come eventually, winter always leads to spring, rivers thaw, darkness disappears with the spark of a match.

He lay quietly in the candle-lit bathroom. The smell of onions and butter coming from the kitchen filled him with a hunger he hadn't felt in weeks. He let his arms float in the oily water, every now and then added more hot to keep the temperature up. He hadn't taken a bath since he was a boy. He could remember being a kind boy, a sweet boy. People would say that in court and it would be true.

PROPER TING

A little girl saw it first. She had been roaming the beach gathering shells, dancing along the water's edge every time a wave hit. Then a mound of sea stuff blocked her path. Strange it was, a bundle of something wrapped in crackling dulse as if ready to be shipped. Under the dark stringy layers were smooth pink limbs that had spent the night tumbling over themselves back towards the shore. It stunk of maggoty fish heads.

The girl screamed.

Two mornings later Mrs Wilcott comes over and knocks. I freeze at the toilet, my stomach seizing up in mid-retch.

"Hallo, hallo," she says through the cracks. "My dear, are you home?"

I wipe my mouth. "Mrs Wilcott, I'm a little busy. I'm leaving soon and..."

"Oh I know, but some awful news there is, I'm sure you heard, oh I thought she knew better, really I did," she says in one breath. "Shall I pour us some tea?"

She pretends that we are only gossiping but I wonder if she came out of mercy because she knew I'd be grieving alone. That's how they are here. I make the tea and try to distract her by apologizing for the piles of clothes, dirty dishes, boxes.

"She should have known better," she says again, "going out in that sea alone. She must have been missing him some bad. Trying to meet him up the bay she was."

By the way Mrs Wilcott looks at me I know we both know that isn't true. By the time she leaves the sky is purple and the tea long cold. I tape the last box and stack it with the others in the car. Most people probably expect me to stay, but they are the same people who want me to leave.

Months earlier, I had knocked on her door to start my interviews and she told me to call her Sinjin. It was her husband I would be wanting, she told me, but he had taken a second job and wouldn't be back for a week or two. Then she told me Sinjin was an old way of pronouncing St John.

"Isn't that a boy's name?" I ask, trying to be polite.

"True enough," she said. "My parents were playing tricks, wouldn't you know. That's the last one, she kept telling him, the last one I swear. My dad didn't see the naked me for weeks. He was right surprised when he did, I tell you."

"That's quite a story."

"It gets better," she said, stepping aside to let me in.

But I had been warned about how people will go on and on if you let them, as if time was just another fish that got away. It was only my first week and already my goal of starting one case study a day had evaporated. "I think I should go," I looked at my watch. "I can come back another time."

"Come now," she said. "Who leaves in the middle of stories?"

I hesitated.

"Okay, here's another. First off, you're pronouncing it all wrong. You don't say it like hope. It's pronounced despair. Bay d'Espoir is bay despair. The exact opposite of what you think."

But the exact opposite of what I thought was that it wasn't normal for her eyes to close in on me like that, like she was both trawler and net.

I went back the next day. She bit her lip as she stepped aside to let me in.

"You've been keeping accurate records of your catches, I assume?" I should have been asking her husband. There was protocol for that.

"Of course," she said, with a curtness I had been expecting. Then: "How about that tea?" She went to the kitchen, her body heavy and strong and lithe all at once. She moved like a dancer, I thought. No, a fish.

I stayed where I was, on the threshold. I was more comfortable with distance. Life should be looked at through binoculars, I wanted to tell her. It is important to stand off, to stay outside the circle. That way you can sort everything out in your own time. You can make your own decisions and draw your own conclusions. Otherwise, otherwise—things can happen.

"Autumn's not halfway started and already you look like three layers of wet wool," she said, sipping. I pulled out my notes, but they fluttered in the breeze of an open window. I couldn't take my eyes off her fingers curling around the cup.

"Is this your first time to Newfoundland?" she asked.

"Yes. This is my first time."

"Well, there's a first time for everything. Don't you think so?"

She squinted at me and I just wanted to say no. No, some things I can wait on. Some things I don't need to do or to see. She nodded her head slowly, to herself, bobbing it up and down like she was under water, her thick dark hair almost floating away. "Maybe I can show you around."

"Sure." But I didn't really mean it. I knew what it was to be a stranger and it had nothing to do with being in Newfoundland.

She showed up a couple of days later with two bicycles. She liked the warm days of September. Driftwood days, she called them. Newspaper-grey days imprinted with the smell of salt. The half-awakened wind through her hair reminded me of when I stepped off the ferry, sea breeze meeting rock breeze like two abandoned lovers. When she told me her husband had been piloting the ferry, my front wheel skidded on the gravel and I fell on my hands, scraping the skin clean off them. She ran me down to the shore's edge and plunged them into the cold stinging water, laughing like it was nothing. I held back my tears, even after the physical pain had long passed. She said he did nothing but work, spending his time either catching fish or ferrying people but that both are the same aren't they, and these days it's more people than fish anyways. I realized that it might have been him I stood beside on the ship's deck in the morning smoke. He had said something about patience, something about waiting and, just as I was about to join in, to respond with something polite and empty, a voice on the other side of him spoke up. And then he and the other man left the railing and went inside. I stayed on deck to watch the sun burn away the fog.

After the news settles, I leave the way I came. This time another captain is at the helm and the sky is clear all afternoon. The sun sets slowly back on the mainland, sometimes reflecting off the asphalt into my eyes, other times strobing from behind the trees. I drive south from Sydney one-handed, shielding my face from the end of the day.

Just outside of Truro, I check into a motel called the Red Sky at Night. I had driven past it at first, but I turn around when I realize I'd been saying *sailor's delight* over and over. I start the next day early and get sucked into the passing current of logging trucks until I reach another coast, then on to half-salted water where the sea begins to narrow and the tides cease. I cross the border into Quebec and slowly I go this time, no faster than the current.

My job was to work with the fish. Not like a proud fisherman, not dredging the sea between here and Norway, lofting the creatures high overhead and smiling for pictures, filling the hold with enough to last a season, carrying them home in a bucket, gutting one in the sink and laying it on a plate. Instead, I visited outports, wharfs and processing plants all along the southern coast, as far away as Ramea and Burgeo to the west and then down along Fortune Bay to the east. I was to count them down and round them off, scrutinize catches and ensure adherence and monitor compliance. Take names and issue quotas, and then report my findings. But I found myself counting curls instead of quotas and reading her expressions instead of ministry guidelines. I started to hear her laughter in the shy morning tide and see the curves of her hips in the hummocks behind the village.

She took to banging on my door at sunrise. "Let me show you what this rock is all about," she'd say. "Just so you know who it is you're messing with."

Monday she brought me to the beach. Tuesday she put a kettle on the stove and showed me old photographs while a bare hour of sun burnt the dew off the grass. On Wednesday she took me up the hill behind the village. She wore big boots and the nettles crackled when she walked. I inhaled details like bakeapple berries, the green-grey matchsticks of moss, the ruddiness of her cheeks, the shoulder where the sweater fell, the long, hard lines of her thighs as we climbed. Birds screeched and she followed the sound, thinking we might have to rescue an animal. I couldn't have cared less about the animals but followed her higher over the ridge, following, just following. She stopped in her tracks and I wondered if she had seen a rabbit or a moose. But she turned around and ran her hands inside my jacket. That was the first time.

The next morning she took me on her boat. I thought that maybe we should talk about him, that maybe we should address this new current, the growing squall, this tidal wave. He was still plying the channel waters, not knowing a storm was brewing in the bay. But I ran out of metaphors.

"Not a word from you," she said. "He has his summer and I have mine. Does it even matter?" She threw the last of the mooring line on the deck, then softened. "Come. This one is my boat."

The *Proper Ting* was small, rusted in parts, its white paint decorated with bouquets of barnacles under the water line. But I was amazed at how big it was once we boarded. I was amazed at how endless the sea was once we were released from land.

I don't know what kind of summers the Indians had. How the fishing was when the English fired at the Beothuk from off the shore. British boats snuck into the bays at night and lobbed delirious cannon shot at anything that moved. Hunted like animals and forced inland, away from the coast's rich resources, the last Beothuk died two centuries ago. That's what she said to me.

"No one is innocent here. Everyone smells of either fish or blood. No wonder the fish are leaving, they were never ours to begin with."

"Maybe the moratorium will bring new life to the province," I offered. "Maybe it's a chance to start fresh."

"You think?" she said. "And are you here to tell me what we're supposed to do, then? Do I retrain as a—as a, what? Do you have a job for me in Ottawa?"

She rose with the cresting wave. She felt too big for me, my line was taut and shaking. The boat lifted and fell in an insistent cadence, like a pulse. I tried again. "There are things you can do. Places you can go."

"No," she said. "And no."

The day will come when there is one last fish and the fishing boats rust.

"Oh come here," she said. "Stop your pouting. Let me show you something." She turned the engine off and grabbed a buoy with a long hook. "I'm going to give you a real task."

She taught me how to pull the net and hold the wheel and watch the waves. She showed me where the knife goes and just how hard you have to slice. "Hold down with your other hand, don't let it slip and don't be afraid of pushing. And quickly, you don't want to lose time." Then she laughed. "You don't want it to remember your face."

She stuffed their white-ribbed holds with summer savory and saved the soft cheeks for me to fry and laughed when I ate them. Afterwards, I staggered at the warmth of her mouth in the wet and spitting wind. The bow rose higher and higher with every wave while the seagulls pretended not to look. That was the second time.

After that we lost count.

It's not that long a drive from Rivière-du-Loup to Montreal, but it takes me all day. She couldn't even swim. Like most sailors and fishermen, she never touched the water. Had I been there I would have caught her, my fingers spreading like a net. I would have stationed myself at the edge of the shoal and herded in the schools of herring and the remnants of cod and the odd trout. Caught in my squid-jigging ground, I would have hauled her up over the side of the dory and gutted her in the dark, one red lantern swinging through the fog.

There is nothing to report now. We dredged the sea, we drained the sea, we emptied it and made it lifeless. That is your report, Minister, spin it how you will. Me, I find a cheap hotel near the Metropolitan highway. It feels odd to speak French, words skirting out of my mouth like tiny crabs. I sleep through checkout time. I sleep all day, voices in the corridors squawking like seagulls. The bed bashing me like a dead carp against the rocks. Nothing hurts in this salty bed. But the fish have teeth and they tear my liver out. If I had known that she was mortal I would have cooked her skin in a frying pan with pork fat and onions. We would have eaten it with a bottle of wine and only when she glanced at the shore would she be reminded of what I had done for us. If I had known that she would die I would have smashed the boat myself.

An outport is a town with only one way out and that is the sea. Roads were eventually built, but not where it counted, not in her psyche. So when he came back into the harbour, he blocked her way.

"Take the road. Come with me," I said to her. "There's no more fish anyways. And you're doing what you shouldn't be doing."

"Ah, you've noticed," she said. "You're smarter than you look."

"Come with me," I said again, floating in a lagoon of hope and promise.

"So you can add me to your findings? Will there be a pie chart for all our kisses? I suppose there will be no moratorium on me, then. Ah my dear, you're sly."

"I'm just thinking of our options."

"They died of disease and despair, you know. They all did. Oh and murder, don't forget the murder."

I didn't understand what she was saying. "Who?"

"The Beothuk." She walked away, her boots galumphing in a way I had grown to associate with wild mornings. "I need to think. I'm going to go think on the sea."

What could I do? I went home and waited. But far off a black wind picked up and lightning breached the iron sky. Shouts ricocheted off the edge of the harbour as a handful of men reeled in their boats and tied them to. After a while I couldn't see the *Proper Ting.*

The wet whoosh of cars wakes me before dawn. I get up and walk south, following Boulevard Saint-Laurent all the way through the city, past the mountain, into downtown, then the old city, till I see the morning sun reflecting off the dull fittings of a ship at dock.

Montreal is an island but it feels nothing of the sea. I buy a sandwich and sit in the park by the river, skeletons of the leafless trees casting spindly shadows behind me. The bag is heavy on my shoulder, a printed draft of my report weighs it down so that it cuts into my skin. Did I mean to bring it? Seagulls and pigeons, bastard family to their east coast cousins, squawk above me. I throw the end of my sandwich over the rail and watch how the birds dive, fighting each other for bits of bread. Obnoxious creatures, they come closer. I pull the first page out of my bag and, crumpling it, throw it over the railing.

They plunge like greedy bombers but spit it out when they don't taste blood. Waterlogged, the page opens up and floats back and forth in the brown frigid swell. This is a game we are going to play. I crumple the next page.

And then the next until the harbour is carpeted with the story of cod. Like at the very beginning, when ecstatic English and Portuguese fishermen could cross the bay just by walking on the backs of fish and when they were done, they fired on the Beothuk just for fun. That's what she told me. The fish were never ours to begin with.

THE SWORDSMAN

Once upon a time a boy wanted to run away and join the circus. He finally did when he was a man, and he didn't run away but was hired, at a very good salary plus benefits, by one of the largest entertainment conglomerates in the world.

But the moment he stepped onto the tarmac, he hated Las Vegas. The air was parched and resentful and, judging by the swimming pools they had seen from the air, it had every right to be. He was taken to an apartment compound where others like him spent their days twisting, turning, jumping, rolling, throwing.

"Nicolai!" A young man in cargo shorts and plastic sandals wheeled in a trolley. "Your swords are in. Heavy bastards!"

The weight of the crate pulled at Nicolai's shoulders, but he refused to let it show; even out of the big top, he liked to play with illusions. The delivery man rubbed a wisp of beard under his bottom lip. He was patient, he liked to watch boxes being opened. But Nicolai pivoted on his heels—a man's swords are his children and are birthed in private. He heard a chuckle behind him. Nicolai was never sure how to interpret these snorts of laughter, this American collapsing of friendliness and mockery in the same chortle. It rankled him.

He didn't have his own room, but the Mingellos brothers had gone back to Greece for their mother's funeral and so the suite was all his. He pried apart the crate's thin boards. Inside, a cardboard box was wrapped in straw. Deeper, tucked under pink Styrofoam peanuts, was a black leather case. He lifted it out and ran his hands over its fine textured surface. The case had two silver clasps: pop, pop. Then oh, the beauty overcame him. The swords lay side by side like lovers asleep in messy blue satin. The silver grips, intricately carved, were thick and solid for optimum handling. A contre-garde embraced each hilt like a woman's hand, a swirl of fingers reaching up and pledging themselves to victory. A card was attached by waxed string and he read the Cyrillic easily: Yemenov, 1915. He had paid a fortune.

He lifted one of the weapons from its resting place. The heft was enormous. He stood up and sliced two rapid, bloodless strokes. The sound of the air splitting in two was magnificent.

Nicolai went to the practice gym after each night's performance. Though the swords were heavy and stiff, he discovered other properties. They were weighted at the tip, an old way of forging steel when a blade was meant to go not just into flesh but through it. The other surprise was the music. Depending on how he sliced and how fast, they resonated different notes, low vibrations in minor keys. When he worked both blades at the same time in the same direction they harmonized, as if one sword was born before the other. He did this over and over just to listen, mesmerized, eyes closed, rocking slightly.

When Nicolai first joined the circus, he looked for the children in the audience. It was how he stripped each moment of fear, rivalries, thoughts of money. Looking for a child that might be him, a boy who barely blinked and hardly moved and dreamed of escape. There were few children in Las Vegas and certainly fewer at this show. What he heard and saw were the women. It was because of the women that he learnt a new word. He had just come backstage and was dampening his face with a towel.

"They sure like to ogle you."

He searched out the voice, looked up. A woman knelt in the scaffolding, an electric cable in her gloved hands. "Yup, there's a few women who will be ordering a long, cool white Russian at the bar tonight."

He was jostled by performers and stage managers but he didn't move. "What's *ogle?*"

"Ogle?" She laughed. "It's a funny word, isn't it? Sounds like a troll. I wonder where it came from, *ogle*. Sounds vaguely Germanic. Not Latin, not with that *g* and *l*. Makes me think of trolls and giants." She stared into the sliver of audience visible from her vantage point. "Never heard of Italian trolls or giants, come to think of it. Just northern European ones. Isn't that interesting?"

Someone hit Nicolai in the back. "Get going, buddy." He wasn't supposed to be there, in the way, in the dark, under the scaffolding as an electrician gathered her cables and wondered about the Germanic origins of a word.

"The women ogle you," she said again, enjoying the sound.

He gathered his towel and knives and looked up but she had gone. A figure moved in the shadows on the next scaffold over.

After a few weeks, he could do all sorts of things with the swords. There was no place for them in the program, however, and no question of replacing the knives with something else. The show had a dramatic arc and the thing about knives was that they could be hidden. For his piece, he'd crawl onto the scene like a beggar, a lost man, and was pounced upon by highway thieves. They robbed him but he pulled out the knives before they could escape.

Slowly, one by one, the blades would flash—from folds in clothing, creases in body—and he'd play with them, taunting the thieves and frightening the audience. The darkness around him would be thick with dread. He'd pretend to hurt himself and double over to look for blood. But there would be no blood and he'd stand straighter or raise his arms to rolling applause. His final act, with the thieves underfoot, was simply cruel. It was something he improvised one night and, after much deliberation, after it was reluctantly admitted that the audience talked about only that afterward, he was allowed to include it. He bent over the thieves and did his work. With his back to the audience he thrust at their faces. The skinny young men always squirmed out of genuine fear. When he finally let go, they stumbled backstage clutching their faces in both real and theatrical agony. He turned to face the audience and quietly picked at his fingernails with the longest of the knives. There was no applause then, only silence. He lingered even after the spot had darkened and only the blade glistened in the expectant expanse of the theatre. It was his favourite moment.

The next time he saw her she was lying on her back under the long vanity in his dressing room. "I'll be outta here in a minute. There was a short and we don't want you killing yourself with your blow dryer."

He didn't know if he was glad to see her, which didn't make sense, or embarrassed, which he refused to consider. "I don't blow dry."

She craned to look. His bald head gleamed with sweat. "No, I don't suppose you do." She grabbed tools from a small kit beside her. "Do you use an electric shaver?"

"No."

"Do you soak your feet in the massage bath?"

"No."

"Do you dream of electric sheep?"

"What?"

"Just kidding." She stood up, patted her legs and dusted off her hands. "Ah, the knife guy. Your piece is macabre. I always have to look away at the end."

"Is not so bad. I save the world from thieves." He thought about *macabre*. He would have to look it up. Probably French, not German.

"That's one way of looking at it." She smiled, it was a warm smile, he even recognized a glimmer of shyness hiding in it. She packed up her tools. "But I guess I shouldn't expect much from a guy who plays with knives." In spite of the softness of her voice, the words were sharp, engraving a line between them as she left. She hadn't fluttered or fawned, or looked him up and down or stretched her body towards him. He called after her. "I have swords. They are much more, uh, delicate. They are old Russian. I have new show, working on new routine. It is much more, much more..." He was at a loss.

"Delicate?"

"Yes," he smiled, grateful. "Delicate. With life, not death. The desert make me want death but the swords are from Russia and I want life."

He wasn't making sense, but the way he raised his eyebrows and looked up at the ceiling when he searched for a word seemed to move her. At the very least, he wondered if she could imagine him without knives.

"I look up ogle," he told her.

"What?"

"I look up and you correct. It is old German, from *eye*."

She squinted, remembering their first encounter. "Oh yeah," she said, "eye. That makes sense." Before shutting the door behind her she warned against plugging too many things into one outlet. Her leave-taking was sudden, wrong even, but he couldn't undo it.

A knock signalled that he had ten minutes before stage time. As the spot followed him onstage and he threw his knives and caught them, someone up on the scaffolding shuddered.

Afterward, he just wanted solitude. Without turning on the lights in the practice gym, he held his swords and sliced furiously until the repetition and droning notes calmed him. His arms fell and he breathed heavily. A low voice spoke out from the other end of the room.

"Delicate eh? Not the first word I would use."

She was on a bench, elbows leaning on her knees. From that distance she reminded him of a lizard between twitches, tasting the air, ready to dart into a hole. It was an odd image, even odder that he didn't find it repellent. She sat up straight, and he thought no, not a lizard. A coyote. Thoughtful, watchful. The desert is full of animals.

"So, knife guy." Her voice was flattened by the room's muddy acoustics. "What is it about deadly blades that you love?"

He'd heard variations of that question before. Intimations of bravado, hints of duels, preludes to seductions. He wondered if that's what she wanted, if she was there to dare or conquer. That was okay, he could do that. But a part of him retreated. He said nothing, waited. Most women fill up the silence with chatter, they lick their lips, or rub their hands along his blades, giggle stupidly about hardness and length. But like the last time, she stood up and walked toward the door.

"Hey..."

"Yes?"

"You asked me—you asked me something."

"You didn't answer."

"But I want to."

She walked toward him until she got within a blade's length. Her eyes were steady and, he was relieved to see, still warm.

"They are frightening to look at," he began, "and they are difficult to work with. And for sure they kill."

She nodded.

He turned the swords in the dim light. "But they sing to me. Old songs," he laughed shyly, "drunken songs."

She didn't laugh, but she didn't turn away either. She was looking at him, into him, as deep as any blade, and he felt seen. It was electrifying. "When I was a boy, I found a knife. It had blood on it. But I wanted no more killing, I wanted to make it dance. I practiced, many hours, many hours. Until that knife was not a killer but a dancer."

"A dancer." Her voice was low, intimate. He noticed that she was beautiful. Her eyes steady, her lips calm, her shoulders straight, her body compact and strong. It was a kind of beauty that could take days to see, and it had, but now that he saw it, he was overwhelmed.

"Would you have a drink with me?" she whispered. He nodded immediately.

He found her house out in the desert, a small, A-frame that seemed like it had been picked up from the seaside and dropped on her street by an ancient tidal wave. She was sitting on the porch when he pulled into the driveway.

"I like to watch the stars," she said.

The tarry black sky was dotted with specks of light, like bits of glass in concrete. Constellations formed, but neither of them knew for certain which ones they were, so they said nothing. Her hand brushed up against his on the bench. She explored the tiny ridges along his palm and wrist that were scars. He watched her and felt content. She pulled him with her to the bedroom.

"Hold on," she asked.

She lit three Mexican votive candles that sat on the window sill. They had been lit and blown out many times before. She left the room and returned with an opened bottle of wine and two glasses. He was eager for sex. He wanted to pull her down, throw her on the bed, scramble over her, devour her, dominate her, and his body trembled with focused anticipation. But something else was at work too. Another part of him wasn't sure he wanted to simply fuck her and leave, but all he had ever done was fuck women and this one was as fuckable as the next. They were in her bedroom and she was lighting candles and pouring wine and he suddenly didn't want to be there anymore. The phrase "make love" had occurred to him that day in the gym, and he had shivered. He had looked away from her intense gaze and his eyes landed on her hands. Now he longed to feel her hands on his face, his lonely face. For the first time in his life, he wanted to know what it was like to make love.

The sulfur smell of the matches singed his nostrils. She walked toward him, a glass of wine in each hand. He put the wine down, took her hands in his, placed them on his face. He kept them there and closed his eyes, inhaled deeply. "We start with the face," he said quietly.

She was Canadian, he found out the next morning, and her name was Paule. It was a man's name but the way she pronounced it was more like *pole*, or even *powle*. He said it a few times. The *l* was soft, the *e* at the end audible only in its absence. She told him that the *e* made it feminine. It was silent and yet it wasn't. When she spoke to him in French, he discovered that, unlike the boxy American language, her language made the hairs on his neck and arms stand up; its guttural vowels and rippling consonants were like a scalding bath. He told her to keep talking and he made love to her again. She laughed at first but he was undaunted, so she talked about Montreal, about skating and ponds and thick beer and crazy friends she left behind. When she ran out of things to say, she told him how she baked bread and the secret to making it rise. Yeast was only part of it, she said, mostly it just takes time. With time you can make anything.

Summer was coming and the tourists were thinning out. The circus crew joked that the only ones they'd see now would be the Russians or the Canadians, tourists for whom hot summers could apparently only be had in foreign locales. Neither he nor Paule found it very funny. They drove to California for a week, finding an inexpensive motel on the sea with smelly towels. He lost her on their first day at the beach. She went in the water and, a strong swimmer but unused to currents, came back to land half a mile up shore. She giggled as he toweled her down roughly.

"I thought you drown." He was angry, shaking. But she laughed so hard she fell down on the sand. "I thought I lost you," he said again. "I was afraid."

"I know," she said. "Isn't that beautiful?"

Sometimes after her shift she would join him as he practised, leaning forward with her elbows on her knees and watching his every move. "Hello Lizard," he'd say, sensing her presence by the way the air moved and pushed up against him. The swords glistened and hummed in the darkened gym, blades thin and deadly with only a translucent sheath of acrylic forgiving his errors. She was fascinated not by his strength or courage but by the shadow of emptiness that coiled around him, and the way he never tried to fill it. The way he courted disaster with every move. The promise of life after death, or perhaps its opposite. One night as he packed his swords he told her he was returning to Russia.

"You're what?"

"It's okay. I go every year, before the season begin again. Visit my family." He pulled the acrylic guards off the blades, careful to tuck in his loose fingers.

"You could have told me. When?"

He looked at his watch, a very old one, his grandfather's, with a tiny window in which the date of the month scrolled by like a pinwheel. "The sixth."

"The sixth? When the fuck is the sixth?"

He never liked it when she swore, but he told himself it was a habit she picked up from the Americans. "The sixth is next Tuesday," he said, trying to set a calm tone for them both. "And then I am back on the twenty-six. Just one week."

She stared at him. "That's three weeks."

She started to say something else. She started to tell him that it was her birthday on the eleventh. She started to tell him that she had planned another trip away, that she was going to drive them up to San Francisco where the breeze off the ocean might be cool and they could wear scarves and sweaters, something she missed. That she had begun dreaming of bringing him to Montreal, walking with him in the snow and waking up on frosty mornings because their child had just jumped on the bed. She started to tell him that when she looked at him, she saw her future, even felt it in her body. She had even planned to tell him about Nina, their years of tumult, the abandonment that left a trench of longing inside her. She wanted to ask him why he hadn't invited her, why he never talked about Russia even after she spent hours telling him everything about Montreal. Almost everything about Montreal. Her eyes grew moist with tears, but she held them back with the force of her jealous belly. Her head hurt, an aching crease over her eyebrows that tightened and tightened. It was like he had woven a spell and was now threatening to break it.

He saw her expression change and was puzzled.

"So. All of August. Fine," she said, and walked quickly out of the gym. He called after her, but she mumbled over her shoulder, "and fuck you."

He decided he wasn't worried. She was a woman and he was Russian. Some things are older than both of them. He'd put his hand on her waist, pull her to him, her back would soften, her chin would settle in his neck. She was a woman and he was Russian.

Every year he went back to Moscow and every year he wondered why. His mother will cry and his father will, within the hour, find some reason to shout at him. His brother will come home after work and they will start drinking. Alexandra will arrive only after his mother has finished cooking, her and Eugene's kids cranky from being picked up late, and she'll sit on Eugene's lap and laugh loudly while she kicks off her shoes and, under cover of the table, settle her toes in Nicolai's crotch. He will glare at her, maybe get up. Maybe not. He'll drink some more and shout back at his father. Later, his brother will pass out on the couch, the kids will sleep in his old room, and he and Alexandra will fuck noiselessly in the closet.

The taxi stopped. The apartment block was one in a row of grey concrete bunkers that had gone up in the 1970s on what had been the outskirts of town.

Streaks of brown marred the building's façade and thick curtains, as if in shame, darkened every window. His mother stood at the stove, scars flattened in the harsh lighting, and his father was lying on the couch watching television, complaining that his wife was doing too much for her circus son. Nicolai knew that his father was jealous of him. It explained everything. As for his brother, Eugene may have escaped their father's persistent wrath, but otherwise he got nothing. Even his wife didn't notice him.

Alexandra brought something new for the closet every time. Little trinkets to hang on tiny nails, glossy magazine pictures to tape up, and now, this time, a small stool she picked up at the parking lot market. It'll make it easier, she said with a wink. And so it did. He could fuck her without the painful strain in his legs and lower back. He never felt his hatred of Alexandra more intently than when they fucked. He could ignore it, and her, before and after. But during, what she took for pent-up passion was a plundering of his own decency. He blamed her for that.

He had forgotten about Alexandra's biting. She said it was the only thing he could take away with him. He usually ignored it, letting the red welts on his neck and shoulder evaporate slowly into the dry air. But Paule's fingers climbed gently up his back—then stopped.

She had surprised herself by driving out to the airport. Nicolai hadn't been expecting it so when he walked through the terminal's gates to look for a taxi the sight of her standing outside her car stopped him short as if he had been struck by it. He was not used to being met at airports. Not used to the presence, the sight, the smell, the smile of a woman he loved. He ran towards her, took a half step like a boy, lifted her into his arms.

"I'm sorry," she said in the car, but he wouldn't hear of it. He told her about the terrible weather, the changing weather, the weather! that plagued him the entire time he was there. She told him about the new acrobats from Korea and the British tourists who vomited in the lobby. The entire family, can you believe it? They chatted animatedly all the way home, hands skimming each other as they spoke. She took him to her place. They bypassed the kitchen where she had a dinner prepared and went directly to the bedroom, the two of them fervent like full-plumed birds. She dropped her dress, he pulled off his shirt. She touched his back. Then backtracked her fingers over the welts.

"What is this?"

He said nothing, he could only look at her as if keeping her attention was like keeping his eyes on the road. He wanted desperately to go forward, to continue. *Don't stop*, he willed her.

But she pulled at his shoulders to turn him around. "What the hell is this?" Then she said something in French.

"What does that mean," he asked.

"Nicolai, what were you doing in Russia?" She narrowed her eyes till he couldn't see himself in them. "Are you married?" It was an absurd question but, once uttered, took on form and flesh. "Are you *married?*"

"Paule! Of course I am not married. Do I wear a ring? Look, I wear no ring."

"Oh wow." She got off the bed and held her dress to her chest.

"*Paule.*"

"I don't believe this." She left the room. "I'm an idiot. Why. Why did I let myself do this. *Tabarnac.*"

He ran after her. "Listen to me. You have to listen to me. There is nothing. There is no one else." He wanted to get everything out. Get it out and lay it on the floor at her feet, a gift of his past, of the worst of everything, and then finally fill himself up with her, only her, only her. "She is just somebody—oh, it is a long story. It is bad. My brother's wife and it happens every time. I hate it, Paule. I hate it."

She turned around. "Your brother's wife?"

Shadows carved across his body, traced contours down his collarbone, his chest, his hips. His skin, a few minutes ago achingly hot, cooled down in the shallow light of evening.

"Yes. *Alexandra,*" he continued. "We were together, not important. Then she married my brother. He works for a bank, not a circus. Much more reliable. I don't love her. But we, we—I can't explain it. It happens. I hate it, Paule."

"You hate it."

"Yes." He ventured a smile; she seemed to understand. "It's not right. We drink too much. Everyone drunk. And then there is the closet. And it happens."

"The closet?"

"She brought a stool this time." He rolled his eyes. "So stupid. A stool."

Paule was calm now, distant. She appeared to him as if at the end of a long and empty corridor. She was impenetrable but he was Russian. Sometimes he could allow himself to remember that he was the star of the circus. A man of knives and invincibility.

"A stool."

"Yes," he nodded, chuckling. "And always she bite me. Like a present. A bite. Maybe two, maybe three." He watched for cues. Perhaps she understood how one is lost in the underbrush, how the stinging nettles reach up and slice against your legs no matter where you turn. Paule's dark eyes comforted him, and he was more grateful than he could ever recall being. He vowed at that moment to be faithful to her and, to seal this promise to himself, brought his fingers to his lips and prayed. Only much later would it occur to him that it may have looked like he was sniffing his fingers, unconsciously remembering the story through smell, and he would have understood her anger even more.

"Everyone drinks and my parents go to bed and the kids go to bed and Eugene passes out. And we go to the closet."

"You have children?"

"No, no! Eugene and Alexandra have two children."

"You sleep with her in the closet."

"No. No, not sleep! Only—."

And here he stumbled. She blinked but held it for a second too long, as if fearful of opening her eyes again. It struck him, in a piercing, flesh-tearing flash, that he was alone with this story. She was neither with him nor in the audience. She was up in the highest girders, barely looking down, just winding up the cables.

"Only what?"

"Only we..." He took a small step back.

"Only we WHAT?"

"Only we fuck."

He was hiding nothing, no knives in his cloak, no swords behind his back. Nothing to stop the curtain from closing. She always saw his weakness. It had made her love him. Not now. Her eyes made one last sweep of the room and landed on the bed. "You have to go now."

He stood his ground. "I stay."

She whirled on him, slashed him across the face with her dress. "No, you do not *fucking* stay. You go."

"Paule! She is nothing. It is nothing." He needed to touch her. "Why you like this?" Panic surged through his body and his fingers trembled as they hovered in the air.

"Maybe how you behave is fine for Russian women. Or even American women. But it's not fine for me. Just leave, Nicolai, and don't come back. *J'ai pas besoin de ça, câlisse.*" She continued to speak in French as he put on his clothes and left the house.

A three-quarter moon lit his way to the main road. The perimeter of the city teemed with wildlife and the more he walked, the more he could feel their eyes on him from behind hedges and under rocks. Between him and the roar of traffic were the sounds of the scurrying of feet and approaching howls. He wondered if vultures flew at night. He hadn't been this afraid of the dark since he was a child. Sweat ran down his face in spite of the cool air. It was all he could do to keep panic from surfacing. But at the same time he stoked the fear, evoked rabid animals, called up images of fangs and sounds of snarls and growls. Better to be afraid of the animals than think of her.

She left his suitcase with the doorman in the lobby of his building. The next two weeks were busy with staging for the new show. Even if they had wanted to see each other, the only available time was at night. Nicolai prepared for his program with a round-the-clock dedication. He imagined she was watching him from the scaffolding, swords rising and falling in graceful arcs meant only for her. Once or twice they passed each other backstage. If she had looked away he could have told himself that it was a question of time and reasonableness. But she looked straight at him and he felt entirely, thoroughly, cruelly unseen.

He ducked out of the pre-show party. As he walked to his apartment, he struggled to empty his mind of the anxiety that had been gripping him. Las Vegas had never felt like home, but he always looked forward to turning off the commercial roads onto the side streets, and then out into his neighbourhood, where auto body shops and grocery stores were as used up as the people. It reminded him of how weary he had grown of gloss and beauty, lights and magic. Some of the faces he passed were familiar and they exchanged greetings. No one seemed to know each other in America, but they acted as if they did. It was something he could live with, he thought, it could be worse.

And then he saw her. He had been unguarded and the blood drained out of his upper body so quickly he grew dizzy. She was standing next to her car, listening to a mechanic in blue coveralls who was pointing to it and talking. A woman he vaguely recognized stood beside her staring into the middle distance. Paule's gaze shifted from the mechanic to Nicolai. Her nod turned to a slow left-right shake of the head. The mechanic was confused but she ignored him. She seemed to steel herself before walking down to Nicolai on the sidewalk.

"Paule," he said.

"Hello."

The sun was behind her, so he had to raise his hand to shield his eyes. He tried to be casual. "Problem with your car?"

"You know, it's always breaking down," she said, then looked away, retracting the shared memory. "I'm just making sure it all works."

"Planning a trip?" he asked with a smile, rhetorically, for conversation, for something to say that would stop him from hurling himself at her feet.

"Yes."

"Where?" He sucked in a breath.

"I'm leaving, Nicolai. I've quit. Nina and I are driving back to Montreal."

Nina, she had spoken of her. Another Canadian, an acrobat. He used to see them together, and then he didn't. His knees suddenly buckled and his arms reached out for support. But Paule was beyond reach. He managed to catch himself and was mortified by his reaction, then angry at her for provoking it. "You are not leaving. What is going on? Paule, why are we doing this?"

But she shook her head and sighed. "Stop it, Nicolai. You can't have everything and neither can I. I've got a post with the Cirque back in Montreal. This is the way it should be. Nina and I, well, you know." She left it at that, just stared at him. Everything and nothing, all at once.

"No..."

She looked away. They were being watched. "I have to finish things with the car."

But she remained rooted. He could have said a number of things. He could have said that he was sorry. He could have told her that meaningless things sometimes have a life of their own, taking on significance the way a tumour takes on dead cells, but that he had excised it out of devotion to her. He could have touched her cheek, willing tears forth like a well dug deep in the sand.

But, forcing a nonchalance that was clearly too painful for them both, he asked, "Why you not stay here and escape the snow?" With me, he wanted to add, with me with me with me. But it was too late.

She said his name, she said goodbye, then something about his swords, something about luck, and walked back to the shop and went directly inside.

He shouted her name but she was lost to him in the dark entrails of the garage. The mechanic came out once and raised his eyebrows, warned him away in the neutral way that men do, by their very presence, inserting themselves like ramparts. Nicolai didn't budge. The sun hurt his eyes. His throat scratched, his head ached. Then a car started—it was hers. It slipped out of the darkness into the white light and rolled past him so close he had to jump back.

He waited onstage in the dark. The music had quieted and the spot searched the floor. He escaped it like an animal, his bare feet sometimes sounding like frightened prey, sometimes like a stalking predator. The light caught him and he whirled around as if cornered. He crossed his arms to grip the swords sheathed on either side of his body. But when he pulled them out the sound made his heart collapse. It was the unmistakable screech of metal sharpening on metal. He didn't have to look to know that the acrylic guards were not on the blades. The music swelled up, a lamenting contralto singing in an unknown language. But he had hesitated and so was behind the music, each grand note a beat or two ahead of his gestures. It created an ominous tension, like a hole at the bottom of a boat that could no longer be ignored.

He wondered if she had done this, or if he had done it to himself. He had only a faint memory, perhaps not even a real one, of sharpening the blades and maybe not covering them. As the edges nicked him and beads of blood welled up on his arms and chest, he found himself submitting to it like a penance. First one edge then the other sliced into the palms of his hands and her remembered how she touched him, the way she had wicked memories from his skin like a sponge. As the blades flayed his arms and legs he thought of her mouth and how it changed shape depending on the language she spoke. A sword flew high, vibrated discordantly with the music, and sliced across his chest. He remembered how she would always look at him as she came, as if knowing he was there was erotic enough.

He fell to his knees. The audience cried out as blood dripped onto the stage from his chest and fingers. How real it all looked. He hoped there would be no children in the seats. Two clowns rushed in with mops, swearing under their breath. They dragged him backstage. The music, his music, continued to play. As he lay in the wings, he understood something. Everything continues, he thought. The music, life, the show. It continues with or without you. Love goes on. It can bring you somewhere or it can leave you behind, but it doesn't really matter, because everything continues anyways. She got in a car and left him behind. She was somewhere in Montreal and he was lying in a pool of blood backstage. It was an odd contrast, a painful chasm, but it was okay. It made him happy. He should have followed her to Montreal, but if he had, he wouldn't be here, drenched and cut and euphoric. Everything and nothing. He closed his eyes and prepared to die.

But he was fired instead. Just like that, the next day. He knew enough about the circus management that there would be no negotiation, no listening to his story, so he didn't bother to try. He cashed the cheque of three months' salary and returned to Russia. Vodka was the only antidote to suffering.

It was a month before he could remove the bandages. He shunned all contact with his family, especially Alexandra, and found an apartment on the other side of town. She was insulted at first and made repeated attempts to see him. In an angry phone call, she warned him that if he ever tried anything with her again she was going to tell Eugene. He waited for her to hang up. She didn't bother him after that. He spent most of his days at a café, drinking espressos and shots of vodka. He showed his scars to anyone who asked. They were impressive—deep gouges in the palms of his hands, slashes up his forearms, nicks in his legs and, lifting his shirt, a thick welt over his left ribs.

"He went to America and came back Jesus!"

It was funny at first and someone always ordered a round of drinks. But then old Anatoly brought his wife.

"She's been sick," he explained.

Nicolai was busy with his glass. "So?"

"Maybe you can—maybe you can touch her." Irini was a translucent grey, he could see she was ill. Underneath her slouch, she looked at him hopefully.

He thought Anatoly was offering his wife to him. Then he realized he was supposed to heal her. That idea was just as ludicrous as the first. "Are you crazy? What are you talking about?"

"You have the marks," the old man said decisively, pointing to Nicolai's hands. Nicolai looked at his palms, then slammed them down on the table. He grabbed Irini by the shoulders and, pushing her out of the way, stormed out.

The next day, they told him, Irini woke up feeling more energetic than she had in months. She had her first bowel movement in two weeks. When Nicolai returned to the café the following afternoon, half a dozen people were waiting for him. A reporter showed up before the week was out. Most days he didn't care. They just wanted to be touched and the free drinks and bread that went with it were a fine trade. It was all a joke until someone brought their baby.

The young mother cradled it in her arms, the father, hardly more than a boy himself, stood behind her. The child was clammy with fever and breathing with considerable effort. They looked at Nicolai with a desperate trust, and it melted his defences. Maybe the last drink had been too long ago, but he couldn't resist any longer: he thought of Paule. He didn't know where the image came from but there was a snow-covered park, a skipping child holding on to her mother's hand. The child's other hand was held by his. *Allez-hop!* they were saying, lifting her high off the ground with every second or third step. He took the infant from the arms of her parents. Paule was rolling a wet ball of snow in thick orange mittens, throwing her head back with laughter. He loved the way her woolen cap was pulled over her ears, the way her brown hair hung out from beneath it. She and the little girl swatted him with snowballs. Nicolai's tears fell on the baby in his arms. The room hushed and quieted. Chairs scraped against the floor as people left their tables to watch. He sucked in his breath and, with no resistance, let out a howl that was heard down the street. He hugged the baby to his chest and wailed. Curious passersby came into the café to see what was going on. Someone took his picture. The baby's fever broke that night.

A week later, someone from the circus emailed Paule the news story. A baby was in Nicolai's arms and he was looking upward. He had grown a small beard but the stubble couldn't hide the lines that ran over his face like dry riverbeds. She saw that he was crying, wailing even. She read the accompanying text about the Swordsman and the people he cured. What nonsense. She couldn't stop shaking.

"Paule, dinner's ready."

She shut down the computer and threw on her jacket. Snow fell sloppily out of the night sky. Standing on her balcony and looking out onto the street, she felt a cavernous inclination to fly to Russia and find him, to pull him out of his drunken stupor and love him. In the crisp dark of the evening, a clarity came over her and, despite the cold air, her anger melted. She thought she had willed him completely out of her mind. But, like a swept floor, he came back dirty and littered as ever. She remembered the way he looked at her, his air of waiting and trusting. The streetlamps cast warm glows up and down the street. It was her favourite time of night, favourite time of winter.

"Paule, you coming? It's getting cold."

NOT BLOOD

On July 15, 1948, the village of Saffuriya turned to dust as fighter jets tore through the sky like comets. While it was the first village shelled from the air, it was not the first to be reduced to rubble. Dust upon dust spread through the land like a benediction and a bomb. As it pierced the valley, the Army was met with almost no resistance; villages whose bones turn to dust so easily do not deserve to be villages, they said.

Three days later, what was left of Saffuriya still remained in the air, dust shimmering like the holy spirit. It is magic, the soldiers said as they passed through pillars of dust that remained on their skin like glitter. On their final night, the infantry celebrated and drank themselves into a stupor, the rabbis sang a prayer, and all of them danced together like stars.

New inhabitants arrived shortly after, arms heavy with baggage and children. Their homes were newly built, boxy and thin, and despite their plainness, more beautiful than they dared imagine. Outside, the wells were still full of sweet water, and the gardens, well-tended and seeded, sprouted as if by magic. This place was given to us by the stars, they said.

The settlers shared everything: the clearing, the digging, the building, the sowing, the harvesting. Eating together in a communal ecstasy, the coal of their stories hardened into diamonds with each retelling. They communicated in a tapestry of several European dialects, and taught each other Hebrew, a language once reserved for the sacred now made simpler for the profane. They learned quickly, the children quicker still.

They loved and even shared each other for a while, thinking this was in the spirit of things. But that didn't last; they were riddled with jealousy and suspicion and even hatred. Unacceptable, they finally agreed, both about the sharing of lovers and the killing of lovers. Yes, one was killed, found drowned in the water reservoir, and everyone knew why and who and how. But they had other things on their mind and said nothing.

Sometimes, as they plowed and planted, they found things in the rubble. The useful pieces were put aside as they waited a proper moment for the past to evaporate. These things are still in thrall to the *shedim*, their *jinns*, the rabbis warned, their devil spirits. Touch nothing. Everything they found was wrapped, stacked, stored and itemized in detail. They touched nothing.

But every now and then, something entirely whole and undestroyed appeared, which is how Rothi found herself with a fully-stocked kitchen. A miracle, she exclaimed, feeling that she had been chosen and rewarded. *Look at these beautiful dishes! These sturdy pots! Look even closer,* she insisted, scraping the rust with her fingernail, *how handsomely they were forged and hammered.*

No one wanted to look. It didn't matter if they didn't believe in the shedim or the jinn or the evil eye—no one wanted to consider that it may have been blood that oxidized the metal.

Rothi had lost everyone. Don't ask when and how or who, she would not speak of it. No one did. It was understood; everything was understood and painful. In Saffuriya, she was given the smallest and the plainest of the homes. It may have even been used for animals. This is paradise, she said. The dusty crate of dishes was proof that her humility was being rewarded. As she pried open its planks and pulled out dish after beautiful dish, pot after sturdy pot, she knew what must be done.

I will cook for you, she said. *I will do this for you. My children, devoured. My sisters and brothers disintegrated. My husband, a collaborator I had to denounce. Who else is there to feed? I will feed you.*

Who could say no? If nothing else, the words *collaborator* and *denounce* left them speechless and reflective. We also did what we had to do, they thought to themselves.

They ate her food—and were shocked into silence to discover it was terrible. Her tasteless, under-prepared, overcooked, ineptly presented food. Stealthily, they began to leave more and more on their plates. And in their napkins, and in the garbage, and fed to the dogs. They learned to fill up at lunch, and sneak into the kitchen late at night. Eventually, this brought a certain camaraderie to the new villagers. There was excitement in shunning, after all, when one was the shunner.

They allowed this arrangement to continue; if nothing else, they were unfailingly polite. What puzzled them most was that everything about the food should have been good, delicious even. The vegetables were fresh, the animals properly slaughtered, the spices freshly ground, the kitchen fully stocked. Was she doing this on purpose? But every evening as Rothi stood in the doorway of the communal hall to watch them eat, her smile only shamed them for their thoughts. Still, it was impossible to chew without grimacing, or digest without regret. New latrines were dug to accommodate the surge.

It is because of the plates, one person said.

The pots are haunted, someone else said.

Look, another whispered, *the dust watches us.*

The laughter that followed was nervous. No one would admit that this was not funny. More and more of them could see that the dust was still hovering in the air, the breeze refusing to take it away. It didn't feel magical, just ghostly. *Who lived here before*, sometimes someone dared wonder aloud. They wanted it to be their ancestors, their gods, their prophets, their dust that danced in the shafts of light that hit just so; dust that was meant to envelop and soothe them.

But no. *Arabs*, was the answer. *Just Arabs*. And someone would spit on the ground and someone else would clean the air with a prayer.

Rothi surprised them all when she put her name in for the next election. Cooking for the village had given her a purpose and a sense of importance. She knew every settler by name and food preference. She knew who was sick and with what and who was having trouble sleeping. But she also knew whose children were a disappointment; who drank in secret; who was cheating on their spouse; who was pencilling in far more work hours than they showed up for; and even who—and there were several—had been stealing from the others. In the weeks leading up to the election, in hushed conversations at the sink or by the gardens, she made sure that each person knew that she knew what she knew. There was no mistaking it, she had something on everyone. It was not a surprise when she won the election for mayor.

She was full of ideas. For starters, all those objects that had been dug up and unearthed then quietly stored outside the village? Those things still dusty and discarded, unused out of suspicion and old-world beliefs? *Bring them in*, she said. *Why are we wasting our energies redoing, refashioning, rebuilding, remaking when everything is already here? It is here for us! We are the rightful users and the chosen owners.*

Within weeks, the material wealth of the village doubled. After Rothi had first pick, the items were distributed equally: beautiful brass headboards and intricately carved baby cots; inlaid furniture and hand-woven carpets; finely sewn jackets and delicate lamps; polished mirrors and regal chairs; malachite earrings and gold bracelets.

The townspeople shook their heads in amusement; rumours that the items were haunted were just silly. Why had they waited this long to recuperate what was rightfully theirs? *This is for us*, they said. *We fought for this, we have lived through hell, we are making the desert bloom!* In that same celebration they inaugurated their new village. It was no longer Saffuriya but Tzippori. *We are here*, they said. *It is ours. This is us.*

But they should have anticipated the maggots. They should have foreseen the infestations. Had they forgotten everything? You cannot leave woven carpets in hot storage and not expect them to eventually pulsate with life.

The rugs were yanked out of their homes and thrown onto bonfires. It took hours. The crackling smell of roasting larvae was unnerving. A few bugs crawled to safety into dark moist corners, and one family panicked that their toddler had been eating them. But for the most part the problem was resolved and Rothi's approval rating returned to normal.

But the village could not rest. The beds collapsed overnight; every single one. Those with brass frames cracked along invisible fault lines; the baby cots were weakened by termites; and the large oak beds, their dark and imposing galleys crafted long ago from passing ships, disintegrated like pulp.

It was to be expected, half the townspeople said, *this land was crumbling until we came along.*

Everything is haunted, whispered the other half.

A week or two after Bedfall, as it was called, the rains came. One by one, the roofs leaked then fractured. It was astounding how roofs that had been there for generations—*generations!*—they were forced to admit—could leak all at once, over their heads, just like this, together, in the same night, under the one rain.

How to explain this? How to even discuss it?

Then everything happened. The sewage back ups. The tomato aphids. Then aphids everywhere. The ants that followed the aphids. The bats that came after the ants, even in daytime. The jackals no longer afraid. The babies lost to jackals.

What can you expect from this god-awful desert country, they said. Where was the milk? There was no honey. There was only rock and bush and poisoned thorns. There was so much panic that weddings were postponed and marriages broke up.

It was Rothi's fault.

Someone had to say it just once for it to be true.

Rothi, whose name when said quickly sounded like *rotten*, had made their town rotten, their affairs rotten, their futures rotten. It was her fault the unpalatable food, the ineffective leadership, the crumbling infrastructure. It was she who dug up the untouchable things, who disturbed the dust until it choked the air. She had made a deal with the devil before and, clearly, she was willing to do it again. They all were, but that was for another day. Rothi had to go. *Now.* No general assembly or even waiting until the next election. Some stood up and said they had *tactics*. This was an emergency. There was rain in the forecast.

In a blur of movement and thunder and falling trees and overflowing riverbanks and restless goats and crying children—days and days and days of crying children! Do we need so many children?—Rothi was taken care of.

That was how they put it and that was enough for anyone who asked.

Within a week, the rain stopped, the animals returned to their pens, the pests flew from the greenhouses, the rashes subsided, relationships were repaired, and their Friday dinner together was an exhalation of laughter. During dessert—a delicious lemon cake, from their own lemons!—a child ran into the dining room and shouted something unintelligible. All they could understand was *rotten* but the mayor had been so swiftly erased from their minds that they looked from their food to the child to their food again, and dismissed him with a wave of their hands.

The child spoke again and this time they understood: Rothi had been found.

That is to say, her body had returned via the river and was floating upside down in the reservoir. A silence permeated the room; even those who had nothing to do with it knew best to keep quiet. A group volunteered to recuperate her body. No one spoke of the bruises or the knife wounds or the traces of poison that were still on her mouth. After a short ceremony, the shortest, Rothi was buried in the communal cemetery.

It wasn't until one of the younger members—of that generation who knew nothing of the necessity of sacrifice and the way one must "bend the rules" to "create the conditions" in order for things to "just happen" so they can "live peacefully" in "their" "holy land"—one of them came forward and suggested that the mysterious death of the town's inaugural mayor must be investigated.

Isak was a budding journalist, and brought out his notepad and pen at the next town council. The elders looked at each other for the briefest of seconds, shifted slightly in their seats, then freely answered all his questions.

That is to say, they blamed it on the Arabs. Oh the clashes, they exclaimed, the night raids, the incessant robberies. The savages who know only violence and who hate us for no reason, who want to wipe us out as others have done throughout our history. To think we came here for peace, only peace! But, G-d help us, we were so successful at keeping the savages at bay that we must have let our guard down. They came at night and took Rothi and we don't want to tell you what they did to her. It is unmentionable. We spit on the ground when we think of her—*them*, when we think of them.

Isak closed his notepad with the gravest of expressions. Now this was a story. More so, this was a story he needed. A young man of big dreams, Isak wanted to work for the biggest paper in the country, in the country's biggest city. It was time to leave this backwater of dust and thyme.

How many Arabs, he asked. *They must have used rocket launchers*, he insisted. *Their women are all veiled*, he confirmed. *Did they behead the mayor?* he nodded.

Yes, a councillor answered quickly, too quickly. She must have been beheaded. Yes, we think she was beheaded.

You don't know? Isak asked. *You did not recuperate the body?*

She was beheaded. The councillors were firm now. *Beheaded.*

Isak could not believe his luck.

The next day, a front-page story ran in *Haaretz. Raped! Beheaded! Terrorists on the loose!*

By week's end, two neighbouring Arab villages were set upon by the Army, the most moral in the world, and flattened. So swiftly and cleanly that nothing remained, not even dishes or carpets or beds. It was done, and what is done is done. Borders were redrawn and hundreds of dunams of rich farmland was dispersed among the townspeople, with the largest portions given to the councillors in recognition of their courage and suffering.

To celebrate, a forest was planted over the unsightly ruins of the destroyed villages.

The first-year anniversary of the newly incorporated and amalgamated town of Tzippori, by now the largest in the northern valley, was a glorious event and attended by everyone from the old Prime Minister to the youngest baby. Soldiers paraded, marching bands blared, and poets exclaimed hundreds of verses. There would have been more verses but the new mayor finally put his foot down.

It was a sunny day of blue cloudless skies as elegant black birds circled high overhead in an embroidery of movement. A breeze from a nearby hill kept them aloft, their wings open and wide as if in permanent embrace. The townsfolk watched in awe as the warm air grew thicker and the birds soared higher. The wind began to pick up and form little eddies of dust around their feet, and then entire pillars of dust on the horizon. Suddenly each person was encased in their own column of air, the dust shimmering on their skin like glitter. The dust was grey then black then red. *Dust devils*, someone laughed. *Magic!*

The wind died down as fast as it had come—*dust season*, someone explained—and a light rain took its place. Then someone held out their arms and screamed. *Blood!* a voice cried. *We are covered in blood!*

As a deep red liquid dripped down their heads, torsos and arms, the townspeople looked at each other and saw endless waves of bloody corpses and crimson monsters. In shock and disbelief, they screamed blood-filled screams. They tore at their own bloody faces, then clawed at each other till everyone was bloodier still. The chaos that followed resulted in one death by stampede, two by heart attack, and three miscarriages. It was also blamed for several divorces. In retaliation, a neighbouring Arab village was immediately destroyed, and the forest planted in its place was said to be the most beautiful in the land.

The one surviving photograph of that day sits in a vault, in a cabinet marked T 1948-1950 B652, in a drawer marked Jul-Dec WG77, in a folder labeled Misc-33-D1. On the back of the photograph was scrawled *Not blood* and signed *Isak Bitton*. His skills for records-keeping were matched only by the need for obfuscation.

THE BEAUTY OF DISASTER

I was on a long stretch of the highway heading back to the city on a clear day in September. Rounding the Sphinx airport, I could see the planes descend one after another, and thought of 9/11. One of the most astonishing acts of revenge on one of the most beautiful days of the month. September is made up of thirty beautiful days, each one as potentially catastrophic as the next. And here, beyond the cloak of pollution that hovers permanently over Cairo, the clarity was mesmerizing.

I don't drive very fast. Driving at or below the speed limit gives you a perspective into other people's desperate habits. It was the clearest day in September, and a car was weaving in and around the traffic behind me. It barely advanced relative to the vehicles around it, and remained visible in my rear-view mirror thanks to its animal headlights and glistening bright green paint. I sucked in my breath and braced for impact as it came up behind me. By some miracle it wove around and settled in front—but a minute later, the weaving resumed. This time the Mercedes (I could see that now) attempted to squeeze into a narrow opening between two taxi vans farther ahead.

Idiot, I thought. What an idiot.

I was used to Mercedes drivers and their BMW counterparts going twice the speed limit on this highway, risking everyone's life and the occasional donkey. No question of tickets or citations, *bak-sheesh* and *wasta* would take care of that. I had no such privilege. Like 95 percent of the country, I swallowed "the bitter pill of wealth disparity" and drank from "vials of colonial poison" and cowered under the "the punishments of infidels." My cousin used to say all that—in English. It was especially on the most sanguine day of September, when the planes rose vertically into the sapphire sky, that I could fathom what he did.

I relaxed again into my interminable drive on this interminable highway. The airport was newly built, a regional hub in the Western Desert that mostly carried tourists to Aswan and Alexandria or businessmen to and from the Gulf. In other words, people you did not want to get into an accident with. But the Mercedes, not as far in front as I had assumed, came back into view. It made a quick lurch to pass a taxi van on the inside. Paid upfront by his cargo of tourists, the taxi's chauffeur would have no reason to go any faster than this leisurely pace. The Mercedes might have made it, but its wheels skidded on a seam on the side of the road, the sun's reflection vibrating on its hood like a strobe light. It began to fishtail.

Ya allah, I murmured and took my foot off the accelerator. The Mercedes spun around to face me, then spun around several times more, coming to a screeching stop by the side of the road, pointing in the wrong direction. By then my car pulled over and had stopped as well, I stopped it I suppose. Our front bumpers were almost touching.

I turned off the engine and jumped out. The close proximity of the passing traffic caught me off guard, and my stiff legs faltered slightly. In a panic of concern, I tried the driver's door handle but it was locked. It took a second or two, but the tinted window finally descended. There was no blood that I could immediately see, and the inside of the cabin seemed intact, as was the driver. It was not a businessman, nor his driver, nor a government official, nor his driver. It was a young woman, at least half my age, upright against the seatbelt and hemmed in by airbags. The family car, clearly. She glanced at me for a quick second but mostly kept her eyes straight ahead. She was alive.

I opened the door and reached in. "Here, get out. You should get out. Walk. Let's see if you are okay. Or don't walk. Are you okay?"

She took a moment to stand up. She had lost her shoes, and her sweatshirt was torn and hanging out over shredded jeans. The traffic alongside was heavy with trucks from the farms and tourists from the airport. Above, the roar of airplanes and the sun in our eyes threatened to obliterate us.

"Are you hurt?"

She felt her body. Patted her legs, moved her feet in circles, looked at her hands, touched her ribs, her face. "Do you see any blood?" she asked me.

I saw a young woman with soft hands and long nails and thin blond streaks in her straightened dark brown hair. She was missing an earring but the rips in her jeans were factory made. No, I shook my head, no blood.

"I guess I'm fine." She almost laughed.

"That's good. What should we do?"

She dove back into her car and rummaged around the floor, emerging triumphant with her phone. "We drive. I need you to drive me home," she said.

I hesitated. *Does she think I am her servant now?* My old Suzuki was in a terrible state—it ferried me to duck farms and chicken hatcheries from Alexandria to Fayoum, and was layered inside and out with dust and shit and grain. Not to mention: her tone was insolent.

I cleared the passenger seat of folders and papers, my work jacket, my work shoes, and makeup bag. "Of course," I said. "You can rest. The seat goes down."

Her eyes shifted around to the back, the floor, the dirty egg cartons, the stained coveralls, and her nose wrinkled. "What is it you do?" she asked. "Are you a serial killer, *yanni*?"

"I am a biologist with the Ministry of Agriculture," I said, thinking this might impress.

Hmmm, she grunted. My words meant nothing to her.

Things happen for a reason, I'm the first to tell you that, and in spite of the accident I felt good about this sequence of events. September is for disasters, after all, and this was a small and manageable one. Also, like the firefighters in New York, I was by some miracle able to help. She leaned against the door, almost curled up, and inhaled deeply.

"I don't need a hospital," she said as if to reassure me.

"We can't just leave your car, we need to call someone," I said.

"Don't worry about it. Fouad will get it tomorrow. I'll tell him to come back."

She didn't say anything after that, just took deep breaths. Breaths that seemed important, I didn't want to interrupt with questions.

She slept, waking only once we got to the bridge at Zamalek and the car was stopping and starting, stopping and starting, traffic and honking getting the better of her. It was after seven and the sky was a dusty pink, a relief from the blue arrogance of earlier, with the puny Cairo Tower visible to our right. Every September, I let myself wonder what it must have felt like to see the World Trade buildings approaching in the distance. Now *those* were towers.

In any case, never let September lull you into complacency. Her phone began clicking like a camera.

"Hashtag accident," she said, smiling broadly.

"What are you doing? Please don't take a picture of me." I softened my tone; she must still be disoriented. "I prefer you not take pictures of me," I repeated.

"Oh come on." She turned around to get both of us in the shot this time. "Hashtag rescue!"

"What is this for?"

"Instagram *yanni*," she said, in that tone which it was now clear she was a master of. "Anyways, it's my birthday."

"It's your birthday? *Today*. Today is your birthday?"

"Yes. Why? Do you want to buy me a present?" She pouted into the cellphone. "Hashtag birthday, hashtag everyone celebrate, hashtag car crash! I was born on hashtag plane crash so it makes sense, right?"

Ya Allah, I murmured several times. At the very least it quieted her down. "So, you are twenty-one years old."

"*Mabrouk*, you are good at math! Well, I guess you would be, *Madame Agricultura*. Are you sure you are not a *zaballa*?" She threw back her head and roared. Calling me a garbage picker was her idea of wit.

I ignored the insult. "I was exactly your age."

"When?"

"Well, twenty-one years ago. When it happened."

She made a little noise, a vague attempt at interest. But her head was back in her phone and her fingers were busy. I do not keep a twenty-one-year-old's attention very long.

As the bridge descended, I asked where she lived and was not surprised to hear Maadi. It was the closest Cairo had to a Western-style suburb. I had been to Maadi exactly once. A cat had fallen out of a tall tree and landed in front of me *wham!* right on the sidewalk. Maadi has actual trees and, apparently, people who keep pets. We stood still, myself and the half dozen people it startled, all of us shocked to be witness to this fatal cat crash. We were as stunned and immobile as the animal—until suddenly it got up, shook itself, and ran away, first under a car, then up the street. We, random strangers all, murmured embarrassingly trite things about luck and nature before going our separate ways. I really mean separate: I changed direction to avoid keeping step with any of them.

I calculated once that I spend almost half my life driving. At least this was a diversion, in spite of the fact that it would delay my return to my flat in the far-flung and godawful district of New Cairo for at least another hour, if not longer. I turned south down the Nile Corniche, direction Maadi, while she did what she could to make herself presentable and clean. She sighed loudly when she flipped down the visor to find the mirror coated in grime. Then there was a rustling of papers as she rummaged around her feet.

"Oh look." She held up one of my reports. "*Duck egg production and incubation*," she read, "*by Rula Atta, MSc*. Is this you?" She held it to her face. "It smells like you!"

"You can please throw that in the back."

But she took a picture of it. "First, can that title be more boring? Second, that's a name to have, especially on a day like today. *Atta. Khalli balak*, be careful, I know things. Most people my age don't. Also, my mother is American. So *yanni*, September 11 is a topic in our house." She laughed. "He was the leader, *Mohammed Atta*. Did you know that? Wouldn't it be funny if you were related!" She leaned forward to look at me. "Resemblance, I see resemblance!"

I did not like the sound of her voice. "We do not look alike," I said. "And of course I know that."

"Oooh." She was drawing conclusions and filling in gaps and making presumptions.

"Oooh nothing," I said. "Tell me where to turn."

"You can put it in GPS," she said.

"Just tell me where to turn."

She gave precise directions which I could not keep track of. At the next bottleneck of traffic I handed her my phone and told her to input the address.

"So were you all arrested?"

"What are you talking about?"

"I heard all the families were arrested and questioned. I can't imagine. Were you tortured? Did they waterboard you? Why didn't you change your name and leave? Not that America would have you haha. But you could go to Cyprus or Qatar. I heard they all went to the Gulf. I'm sure there are duck farms in Qatar too," she laughed loudly. Then she looked over at me with a stare I could almost physically feel. "I mean it was the worst terrorism ever. *Ever.*"

"Is that what your mother says?"

"My mother works at the American Embassy so if anyone knows anything, she does," she said without a trace of irony.

This information intrigued me greatly. Embassies taunt us with visas and favours and money on long, long strings. But I have never encountered anyone who actually worked at an embassy. I know professors of course, and farmers, and once, in an elevator, met the owner of Daoud Poultry, the largest hatchery in Fayoum. He was not polite.

"What does your mother do?" I asked her.

"At the embassy? I am sworn to secrecy," she laughed, and mimed sealing her mouth. The vow lasted all of one second. "She's a diplomatic attaché." She lowered her voice for dramatic effect: "If you know what that means. And if you do, I will have to kill you." I expected more laughter, but none came.

I knew that diplomatic attachés existed outside the rank and file of diplomatic missions and could have any number of covert mandates. I knew that Egypt was full of shifty attachés with greased smiles and envelopes of money. I also knew that her mother would be remarking on the blue skies of September.

I wanted to change the subject. "What does your father do?"

"He's a professor at AUC, he teaches politics."

"He's Egyptian?"

"Yes, but he has an American passport now."

"Lucky him."

"That's what he says. Anyways, they're snorkeling in the Red Sea. That's why I was at the airport. Fouad our driver was supposed to drive them but he is in Tanta because his mother is sick or something I have no idea. He needs to come back. I'm still learning to drive," she laughed. "But you won't say a word of this to anyone. Right?" Once again, her stare held an unexpected force, it was not something I was used to experiencing. "Anyways, with a name like yours you don't want to draw attention to yourself," she added in a tone that she must have heard her mother use. "It's best if people like you stay out of trouble."

I was taken aback, not sure if she was playing with me or scaring me. But then in a sing-song voice she sang a stupid line from a popular Chipsy commercial: "*Mish kidda walla eh!*"

Maadi was like the rest of Cairo if you removed every second street, doubled the number of trees and parks, and built only large villas and tidy apartment buildings. Not a donkey or goat in sight. By the time we arrived at her house I was weary of her company. But I was also just weary and needed to use the bathroom, so when she invited me in I suppressed the refusal expected of me, and accepted.

It was a large villa behind a short stone wall with a metal gate and a well cultivated garden. "Does your mother like gardening?" I may have asked that question just to hear her scoff, and she did not disappoint.

"My mother most definitely does not do her own gardening," the girl said. "She likes gardens, not gardening."

I then had a thought that I couldn't resist saying out loud. "Funny your parents are away on your birthday?"

She looked at me with an accomplished mixture of defiance and newfound independence. "Not funny at all. Maybe you have never heard of ... parties?" Her laughter stayed in the room long after she left.

I waited alone in the large front room until an old woman in a threadbare galabaya came running and introduced herself. Saida offered me tea and showed me the bathroom. The girl returned several minutes later in a set of new clothes in the same uniform: jeans and a sweatshirt, this one emblazoned with the word Yale. She did a double take as if surprised I was still there. "Would you like some money? Can I pay you for your trouble?" she asked, clearly flustered by the inconvenience of it all. "You were a great help, thank you." She put a hand on her heart in the most false gesture of humility I had ever seen. She called for Saida again, who led me to another room. I never saw the girl after that.

I am rarely the recipient of baksheesh but admit to paying it without a thought. I had to wonder if I, too, had exhibited the subtle but very palpable contempt of which I was now the beneficiary. Saida opened a small safe behind a small door in a small ornate side table and after a few seconds of inspection, took out a roll of bills. Then she too left me alone, presumably to leave at my leisure. The wad was tightly wound and heavy in my hands. Was it small bills wound into an impressive roll, or large denominations that would pay for a year's expenses? I knew the amount would reflect my importance relative to the girl—or the threat I posed to her comfortable existence. How much money would someone like me demand? How much would it cost to keep me quiet about the accident? Those were critical questions.

It was less money than I expected. I pulled over just before getting back on the Ring Road and counted. Although I was happy to see an American hundred-dollar bill thrown in for good measure, the total amount was not something a family like hers would miss or even take notice of. It was enough for a weekend in Port Said at a two-star hotel, or a month's rent for a tiny flat like mine. Or both if I was ridiculously frugal. There are three classes of people in Egypt: poor, pretend not poor, and expat. People like me are debris on the Red Sea floating between the first two.

I am not a greedy person, but I'd never been to the Sinai, let alone to snorkel. I'd never owned a car that wasn't already a decade old. Mostly though, I'd never left the country. Never been on an airplane, never dared dream I could. Words like airline and passport and departure gate and cruising altitude—what did they mean? They frightened me, to be honest, and had led to only disaster. But I suddenly wanted to experience them. As I steered my car back into the trembling traffic of the city, I was pierced by hope and longing with such a violence that it made me collapse with sadness. Like an imploding tower.

Then my body was thrown against the dashboard and an angry horn scorched my ears. A car—gleaming and clean, a BMW I immediately noted—was jammed up against mine, its right bumper embedded in my left bumper. The driver jumped out screaming, already on his phone, looking around like a beacon for a police officer or a mercenary thug. Was I to blame? He insisted I was. He inspected the very visible scratches on the brilliant paint and looked at me with disdain and contempt. That look. He wanted my name, the name of my husband, my address, the name of my employer. It wouldn't be long before the police would show up and I could easily be detained, or worse. Not only that, any whiff of legal troubles and the ministry will send me packing. I had literally no defence. Except money. I gave him all the money. He sighed and made a feeble attempt to say something, but I didn't care. He returned to his car and I to mine.

Some disasters are necessary and important. They help to shift the world, rearrange it to something more understandable and fair. It might settle back eventually, but for a moment there is connection and an opening and an ever so discernible difference in how the sky looks. Or maybe disasters pretend to be about change but only begin and end in nothingness. They mock us with their transformations, they confuse decay with progress. Disasters wear us down.

By the time I got home, my flat was dark and I was exhausted. It was as if all the disasters in the world had flown right through me in a few short hours. I had just enough energy to search the faculty at the American University of Cairo and send the Mercedes girl's father an email. There is no excuse for reckless driving on the highway, I wrote, and I should be properly compensated for his daughter's foolishness, my inconvenience, and the extensive damage to my car. Luckily for all involved, I added, it was a beautiful day in September and you could see for miles, and so we were able to avoid complete disaster.

I signed it, *Rula Mohammed Atta*. It is a name that will frighten him, if not his daughter.

ACKNOWLEDGMENTS

I am absurdly lucky to be surrounded by a bounty of family, friends and communities. It wasn't always this way, and I am frequently in a state of astonishment. My girls are now grown up, former lovers are lifelong friends, and everything feels meaningful and urgent. More than anything, this is for Samia and Emma. Your future is everything to me. And for Colleen Ayoup. Contentment is not overrated; it is love at its kindest.

Thank you to my publisher, Robin Philpot, who has trusted me with a few things recently. I hope I do not disappoint. Thank you to Elise Moser, Samia Marshy and Anita Anand for your insightful editing. Thank you to the Quebec Writers Federation, who never fails to reminds us that what we do is important, or at least can strive to be. Thank you to the Canada Council, we are lucky to have you. Thank you to Montreal for your bike paths, free swimming pools, glorious parks, abundant libraries and verdant markets. As much as I *sit* to work, living in Montreal has meant I can also keep on moving, fabulously so.

Finally, I'd like to acknowledge the people of Gaza and Lebanon, and all those who have been advocating for the peace, security, and humanity of Palestine and the Palestinians. May we see truth, reconciliation, and justice in our lifetime.

Versions of the following stories have been previously published:

Ramadan (*Telling Stories: New English Stories from Quebec*, Vehicule Press)

Winter, *Water, the Waiter* (Danforth Review, No. 78)

A Thousand and One Nights in Palmyra's Bed (Best Canadian Stories, Oberon Press)

Hamdo the Hero (Danforth Review, No. 41)

The Job (Fireweed, No. 73)

The Plow (Danforth Review, No. 65)

ALSO FROM BARAKA BOOKS

LOOKING FOR HER by Carolyn Marie Souaid

SAINTS REST by Luke Francis Beirne

DEAR HAIDER by Lili Zeng

THE THICKNESS OF ICE by Gerard Beirne

EINSTEIN ON ISRAEL AND ZIONISM,
NEW ENRICHED EDIITION by Fred Jerome

A JEW IN RAMALLAH AND OTHER ESSAYS
by Carla Blank

EYES HAVE SEEN, FROM MISSISSIPPI TO
MONTREAL by Fred Anderson

MIX
Paper
FSC® C100212
www.fsc.org

Printed by Imprimerie Gauvin
Gatineau, Québec